"What a gut punch of a book! Very well written and impossible to put down…"
--James Reasoner, *New York Times* and *USA Today* bestselling author

THE HORSE (1863)

A Novel

JAMES CICCONE

The Horse
Copyright © 2024 by James Ciccone
Cover Design: James Ciccone
Wang & Jean Publishers
Subsidiary of Average White Press LLC
244 Fifth Avenue
Suite C250
New York, NY 10001

ISBN: 979-8-218-30960-2

This book is a work of fiction inspired by actual events. The characters, incidents, and dialogues are products of the author's imagination and are not to be construed as real.

No part of this book may be used or reproduced in any manner whatsoever without written permission of the publisher, except in the case of brief quotations embodied in critical articles and reviews.

All rights reserved, including the right to reproduce this book or portions thereof in any form whatsoever. For information, address Wang & Jean Subsidiary Rights Department, 244 Fifth Avenue, Suite C250, New York, NY 10001

For information about special discounts for bulk purchases, autographed copies, media inquiries, fan mail, or to book an event, please contact Wang & Jean at 646-353-8086.

BOOKS BY JAMES CICCONE
A Good Day to Die (2020)
Stagecoach Justice (2021)

For My Father

na jaayate' miriyate' vaa kadaachin naayam bhuthva bhavithass na bhooyah: ajo nithyah saasvato'yam puraano na hanyate' hanyamaane' sareere'

"The past is never dead. It's not even past."
--William Faulkner

"Fight for the things that matter."
--Compton T. Dodson

The Horse

August 14, 1871

The Adelphi Hotel
Saratoga Springs, New York

TO WHOM IT MAY CONCERN:

My name is Alexander Whitfield Holmes, and this is my confession. In August 1863, I killed the champion racehorse Lizzie W and hid her body under a haymow close to the spot where she went over in her stall on the Saratoga Race Course. Henry Freeman, a colored groom from a nearby barn, aided me in the crime, although at first he tried to talk me out of it. I coerced Henry into helping by threatening to report his love affair with an underage girl to the local authorities if he refused to cooperate. The 13-year-old girl was pregnant at the time. Fearing the worse the law offered a colored groom in his predicament, which was a lynch mob, Henry was motivated purely by fear to swing into Lizzie W's stall with Derringer in hand. While the assault was underway, the filly, appearing to sense her own mortality, revolted. She whinnied, flashed the wild white of her eyes, reared, and beat the air with her hooves, until a single gunshot blast to her head settled the matter. All fell silent after that. In spite of that silence, the story didn't end there, not by a long shot.

The controversy that led to this horrific act was the success the three-year-old filly achieved on the racetrack and the ownership dispute that followed. Mr. Charles Ogden Tripps -- a man who made a fortune in the Philadelphia money market, but knew absolutely nothing about racehorses -- agreed to become my partner. The terms were simple: He would put up the cash and rely on my instincts to select a yearling at the Lexington Tattersall's Select Horse Auction, and I would develop the horse into a legitimate stakes-quality animal, a racehorse capable of winning at Saratoga. In fair exchange for this service, I was given fifty percent of the horse. Mr. Tripps said he was willing to pay full price to meet the demands of the enterprise.

Like any gentleman of his stature, Mr. Tripps wanted to win at Saratoga more than anything in the world. When I confessed that I had no money to invest in the proposition, he said the gift of understanding the mysteries of racehorses I offered to the operation was considerably more valuable than any amount of money a man of my pedigree could ever hope to raise in a dozen lifetimes.

"You have a gift," he confided, pulling the cigar out of his mouth to expand the point. "Unlocking the mysteries of horses to the point where their feet absolutely fly over a racetrack is a tall order, isn't it? I have no idea where a gift like that comes from. Do you?"

He drew smoke from the cigar, savored it, examined the cigar's length, and looked past me to the horizon. A man as powerful as Mr. Tripps never expects a response from a member of any of the subordinate classes. He had the credit and leverage to bid on any of the horses sent through the sales ring that he fancied, and I had the talent and patience to get them to the winner's circle. This was a perfect match, sort of like a pair of Etruscan cups stacked one on top of the other. According to the terms of our oral agreement, the instant the auctioneer's gavel fell, and Mr. Tripps fronted the cash to complete the transaction, my fifty percent share of the horse vested, and the contract was binding even before the horse walked off the grounds. The plan was perfect in all respects, except I would later learn that no plan is perfect, particularly where, as here, it relies on a horse trader for its authenticity.

I examined the pedigrees of the yearlings listed in the sales catalogue, picked out Lizzie W from a small group of horses with promising crosses or nicks in their pedigrees, inspected each aspect of Lizzie W's conformation, including her forelegs, knees, back, the length of her neck, the size of her nostrils, the color of her feet, the dip in her back, the size of her barrel, her withers, and the sweep of her elegant legs as she walked professionally without winging out, and declared her sound. This filly was our target. She was the one horse in the entire sale likely to develop into a champion, an analysis that required expertise, experience, and plenty of luck. Mr. Tripps used this information to trigger what turned out to be a bidding war.

A stylishly dressed negro groom wearing a black waistcoat, a fancy black derby, and white gloves, the kind of gloves used by butlers to wait tables or pall bearers to steady caskets, calmly posed the filly under the hot, white lamps trained on the sales ring. The smell of the negro groom's hand against the horse's muzzle was obscured by the gloves so not to disturb the horse's composure. The sales ring was enclosed by velvet ropes and polished brass standards. A cloud of blue cigar smoke hung over the audience.

The excitement in the room matched the spectacle that attends prize fights or presidential debates, yet Lizzie W did not rear or show any signs of nervous energy whatsoever. Instead, there was a presence that was gorgeous and regal and arrogant in the way the chestnut filly was led into the ring. Her ears twitched. She stopped, stood at the center of the ring, and stared at the adoring audience and beyond as if she possessed an extra sense, a survival instinct the other beasts that had passed through the sales ring that evening did not share. The groom pushed the filly's right shoulder while holding the shank, so the whole assemblage of horse flesh took a single backward step before continuing to stand professionally.

The filly had been broken, prepped, and groomed for the occasion. Every hair on her body had been brushed to brilliance. Her tail had been combed and clipped. Her hooves were polished to perfection. Her conformation was absolutely stunning, even flawless.

The line over her hips and across her back was indeed flawless. It resembled the graceful swoops and dives of free birds gliding on pockets of air. The line did not suggest the deep curvature of a swayback. Instead, it assumed the correct angle of a pleasant, gentle arc, the kind of arc capable of producing raw speed without breaking down under the rigors of training. Lizzie W seemed to announce her perfection through the arrogance of her posture. Mr. Tripps was smitten. The adoring crowd of bankers, lawyers, cattlemen, industrialists, and other gentlemen, the staples of nearly every sector of society, was smitten, too. Grown men in conspiratorial groups murmured at the first sight of her.

Although only a yearling, the chestnut had already begun to fill out and stood over fourteen hands with a white blaze and one white stocking. Unlike the other stock in the sales catalogue that made it through the ring that day, Lizzie W was considered a lock to show speed and stamina over a distance of ground. With this in mind, the bidding war began.

The auctioneer's rhythmic chant unleashed a cascade of hoots and hollers from every quarter of the audience. The groom turned the filly in a tight circle to influence the bidding. Then, he asked her to stand.

Lizzie W complied intelligently, not merely standing without molestation, but absolutely posing, ears stiffly erect, tail flat and still, eyes peering knowingly into the darkness that bathed the audience. Her coat was dappled and caught the light just so. The horse had an unmistakable presence. She appeared to realize everything that was at stake in that ring, including the money.

The price rose. The men raised their hands, hooted, and hollered. The groom turned the horse again. The auctioneer pressed the audience for higher bids. The crowd complied. Ownership of the prized racehorse remained in doubt.

Mr. Tripps dismissively raised his right hand as if to signal to his competitors that they need not challenge his authority or prolong the inevitable. He was a bully. He had a habit of winning whatever he lusted after, whether it was a woman, a fine painting, an expensive bottle of wine, anything, and he lusted after Lizzie W. Nevertheless, his attitude didn't put a stop to the bidding war.

While the negro groom yanked the shank with one hand and pushed the filly backward one step with the other hand, the bids continued to rain down upon the proceedings from all areas of the audience, inspired, in part, by the auctioneer who barked and cajoled and exhorted the gentlemen to raise their bids ever higher, and, in part, by the filly's inherent beauty and power. The auctioneer's musical chant intensified and ignited still another wave of nervous competition across the audience, a bona fide bidding war.

Lizzie W menacingly bowed her neck and pawed at the wood shavings on the floor as if to charge, as if she understood the contest. Everything about the filly that wore hip number "218" plastered to her rump confirmed my decision to buy her. She was an athlete, a champion with an indomitable will inherited from her ancient bloodlines. I leaned close to my partner's ear and whispered my approval, so Mr. Tripps did his part.

He made an extraordinarily high bid of $5,000 that shocked the audience into a stunned silence. It was the highest price of record ever paid for a racehorse. The gavel fell. The bidding war was over. He had won.

Mr. Tripps wore spectacles, a vest over a snowy white high collared shirt, and a finely tailored black waistcoat. He was the sort of pushy young man you'd expect to see working as a barrister in one of the grand courthouses in Philadelphia or New York, the courthouses with granite columns, ornate woodcarvings on the interior walls, long marble staircases, and high domed ceilings, but he was actually a wealthy cattle rancher from Eagle Pass, Texas, a sort of nomad's land near the Rio Grande, a perfect hideout for outlaws, a place the law and the railroads hadn't reached yet. There were thousands of head of cattle on his Sunrise Valley Ranch. The spread was endless and unfenced. There was grass everywhere for his cattle to graze on across the vast plains, his plains. His cows got fat enough each fall for the ranch hands to crowd them into railroad cars and send them off to slaughter. When Mr. Tripps's ranch hands weren't busy crowding railroad cars with cattle, they were busy elsewhere, keeping herds from stampeding at the sight of wolves, branding calves at roundups, standing watch at night for cattle rustlers, work like that. The only thing Mr. Tripps enjoyed more than shipping his cattle off to market each spring was beating Yankee investors in a bidding war. It had been a good day to buy.

The Horse

Mr. Tripps, as usual, kept the pearl handle of his expensive Derringer concealed beneath his vest. I never saw him reach for it in times of conflict. Instead, he confidently pushed his hat away from his forehead. This was usually all he had to do to make folks respect his authority. It was his way of reminding the world who he was, and if the world disagreed, it was his way of advising the world that it was smart to reconsider.

He was the type of man who had gotten used to getting his way just by clearing his throat, whether it was at an auction, the feed store, the train depot, church, or anywhere. And when clearing his throat didn't work, he opened his bank roll to settle the matter. That always worked. It worked in the sales ring that day.

I took a fistful of the shank away from the negro groom and led the filly away from the sales ring with Mr. Tripps in attendance. He walked hurriedly alongside to keep up. The filly tossed her head rhythmically about as she dragged her hooves along through the dust. Even as she tossed her head and flicked her tail at flies, she didn't forsake the regal fluidity of the strides she inherited from her majestic bloodlines.

We were both quite heady in that victorious walk with our prized racehorse and agreed to sell her on the open market after she acquitted herself on the racetrack and split the proceeds at the appropriate time. This, of course, was a long way off at this point. I knew of the challenges ahead to train a horse of this caliber in the wilds of upstate New York, and I wish to emphasize that Mr. Tripps's passive share meant he could not legally sell, divide, devise, give away, or alienate my ownership interest in any way without my consent.

These details may seem ironic, considering the filly no longer lives, and I know what is making the scratching and gnawing sounds in this hotel room, the sounds behind the walls, above the ceiling, and outside the window, and I am fully aware that I will no longer be haunted by these sounds whence my life is finally over. I wonder if what awaits me in the afterlife can possibly be worse than what happened at Saratoga that summer, even if it turns out that the lowest House of Hell rages with grease fires that lick at my flesh, the stench of one thousand buckets of piss overwhelms my lungs, the poison of a busy retinue of raccoons gnaw hungrily and mercilessly at open flesh wounds over my exposed bones, the noise of swarms of busy mosquitoes bedevil me, and the bitter pleas of souls as wretched as my own are my only comfort in a state of eternal confinement.

If a judge had relegated me to the simple justice of being rudely urged across an empty stage to face a jeering audience whistling insults at the trap on the

The Horse

gallows and the ignominy of a hangman's noose placed spitefully around my neck like a strange necklace, the sentence would have been far too generous and humane to avenge the look of shocked outrage and terror that crossed the filly's face when it became plain to the beast that betrayal had visited her stall. This was strictly a case of iron breaking bone. It was not a ritual or an accident. It was a revenge killing and nothing more.

****

I argued constantly with Mr. Tripps over the progress of the filly during the spring and summer of 1862. I am positive my piercing green eyes showed my anger during those arguments. I acquired the disturbing habit of staring a lot as a child. Whenever I became upset later in life, I fell into the old habit of staring, and this made me seem dangerous, even criminal.

If I had to guess, I would say somewhere in that stare is where the Evil Man resides. Just as I was convinced the filly was a champion, and this destiny was ordained by her ancient bloodlines, so, too, was I convinced the Evil Man was growing inside of me, a curse I inherited from the mystery of my ancient bloodlines. I was sure of it. Of course, I didn't have proof, but I didn't need it. I knew the odd stare, spell really, that haunted me from childhood was connected to the Evil Man.

The public side of my personality could empathize with Mr. Tripps's argument. It was not easy being patient. It was less than easy being patient when you paid the bills. However, the Evil Man growing inside of me was not quite as rational. The Evil Man was anxious to rebel against Mr. Tripps's impatience. The Evil Man hated Mr. Tripps and all that he stood for, including his insistence that the filly mature and produce immediately.

The filly was two-years-old and still very green. On the farm, we had the advantage of jogging her over hill and dale and through the rough going in the woods. Unlike horses trained on the flats, this should have built stamina and made the filly early. It didn't. She still wasn't particularly interested in racing, and she hadn't yet proven to be a particularly good mover on a racetrack.

The exercise boy had difficulty even bringing her to a gallop in the mornings. She playfully tossed her head during the gallops, watching everything around her that moved, whether it was a bird opening its wings overhead or blades of grass flickering in the wind, instead of simply dropping her head against the bit and focusing on the business of moving forward down the race- track. I climbed on her a time or two myself without much success. Nothing worked.

I repeatedly implored Mr. Tripps to take an interest in the filly's progress, but he never so much as got a speck of mud on his shoes for the two years it took to get Lizzie W to Saratoga. He never set foot in the barn, never visited Lizzie W's stall, never appeared to take more than a perfunctory interest in the operation, never seemed to care. He only cared about winning and winning immediately. He was one thoroughly arrogant man. He steadfastly refused to fund the operation further. He breached his promise.

When I asked him if he truly cared about the welfare of the filly beyond what she might be able to achieve on the racetrack, or what she meant in society as mere decoration, he said the filly meant nothing more to him than any of his other financial investments, and it was my job to worry about the small things that happen on the farm. I explained to him that each horse was different and the filly would take more time to become fit and ready to race. I begged him not to give up hope. He dismissed the overture as the sign of impending failure, a matter that insisted that he cut his losses. That's when he stopped paying for feed, hay, bandages, shoes, and everything else associated with the filly's upkeep.

Honestly, I thought of going to the Law. I was convinced any fair-minded judge would enter judgment sustaining my claim, enforcing the terms of our agreement, and protecting the welfare of the innocent animal. Yet something held me back. I was afraid of Mr. Tripps's connections in the political realm, and it t'was I who imagined that those connections ran straight to the purse strings of any judge in the land, and what practical chance would a lowly down on his luck horse trainer without a penny to his name have of convincing a judge, or really any other politician, to enforce the terms of a horse trade without iron clad paper work, and against a man as powerful as Mr. Tripps, and the skeptic inside of me held me back. Henry, the negro groom, knew of my troubles, too. Henry was aware that I had little confidence in the fairness of such a contest, particularly against odds as long as those.

I believe a different man, a stranger, emerged out of me in the spring of 1862, when the winter snows were still draining off the hills, at the point I had decided the law was not a viable option. The Bible implores us to be on guard against covetousness, for one's life does not consist in the abundance of possessions, but unlike the greedy man, the Evil Man, the conniving man, the vengeful man inside of Alexander Whitfield Holmes

The Horse

broke that code, began to covet all sorts of worldly things, and had already decided the filly's fate.

I was not a monster. I persisted in the filly's best interests. Unfortunately, the filly had its own time clock to observe. The horse promptly bucked shins the first time we got her to breeze over a length of ground. This was still another setback. It wasn't fatal, but it was a setback nevertheless, and setbacks cost time and money.

The setback meant that she needed more time to grow into her frame. Her bones were still green. She needed more time to mature, and I was determined to give her all of the time she needed. I had no choice. I never lost faith in her championship mettle. Moreover, I had grown attached to the horse and began to treat her like one of my children, though I never married and had no idea what it felt like to raise a child of my own.

When I asked Mr. Tripps what we might do with the money if the filly became a champion at Saratoga and we sold her as agreed, since he was a businessman preoccupied with financial matters, he reiterated that we would split the proceeds evenly and go our separate ways.

"I am a busy man," he said. "Do you expect me to actually set foot in a barn? That is why I hire help, isn't it?"

Mr. Tripps could simply have kept his word and honored our agreement, and the filly would still be alive. However, instead of keeping his word, he elected to exploit the one hole in the arrangement to his personal advantage. The foal papers on file with the Jockey Club was the only writing that purported to prove ownership, and that document registered only one person as the filly's sole owner, Charles Ogden Tripps. Our gentlemen's agreement was not in writing. It was based solely on a bill of sale and a handshake, which was the custom of the day.

In the two years it took to develop the filly into a racehorse, Mr. Tripps reassured me again and again that our agreement was solid, yet he never offered to pay another cent. Again and again, I told him of my dream to win at Saratoga and use the proceeds of the sale to buy a farm, acquire my own string, maybe ten head or so, and put all of my troubles behind me. He gave me every assurance that we had a meeting of the minds.

I dutifully rose before the sun each morning to attend to the horses, walk them, gallop them, bathe them, muck out their stalls, put down a bed of fresh hay, alfalfa, and buckets of cool water. Still, we had to take our time and let the filly mature. I had other horses in the stable to attend to as well.

The Horse

Early one morning, Henry and I hung over the rail and watched horses from other stables train. I can close my eyes in this hotel room and still hear the air blasting out of the nostrils of their mounts. The mist still hung over the ground, and opportunistic gulls wheeled in the air. The boys pressed the toes of their riding boots against the irons, and their backsides barely touched the paper-thin saddles fastened to their galloping mounts.

"These are some very fast horses. What are you going to do to make our filly run fast like that?" Henry inquired, leaning against the rail with a blade of straw in his mouth.

"Poison ivy and Mother Nature."

"Poison ivy!"

"I do roughly the same thing other trainers do, except I am smart enough to get out of the way of Mother Nature, first and foremost. I stay in my place and try not to over train the horses or make them forward. In other words, I take my time. I do not rush Mother Nature. You cannot rush a horse, just like you cannot rush a flower to bloom. You cannot rush a racehorse to run fast. If you listen to them, careful and slow… eventually they will tell you when they are ready to run. But you have to take the time to listen to them first and mean it, my friend. They know when you don't mean it. They still have all of their natural instincts, even when society has robbed us of ours. Desperation is the enemy of achievement. Patience is its friend. Achievement is all that matters on a racetrack, either you win or you don't. Horses love running. It is in their blood. If a trainer is wise, he will gently guide a young horse's progress and give them time to do what they are born to do. The trainers who fail are the ones who make the mistake of insisting that the process follow arbitrary deadlines that have nothing to do with the clock that Mother Nature placed in each one of these animals. The mistake of impatience is the one that makes them lame, makes them prone to hidden breathing problems, causes sore feet, or makes them downright ornery and contrary, and impatience is the mistake most likely to make them drop out of contention in a horse race. After a while, the good ones get wise to what the game is out there. Simple. Once you get there, and it ain't easy getting there, and you have been patient with them, the real secret is to feed them poison ivy. I am going to feed that filly as much poison ivy as I can get my hands on."

We walked back to the barn.

"How will poison ivy help our case? How will it make the filly fast?"

"It won't. The filly loves the stuff. It numbs her better than any narcotic you can get your hands on.

The Horse

It helps her breathe better, get more air into her lungs when she runs. It keeps the soreness away from her legs. She don't feel no pain on it, you know what I mean. I can train her on it. I can race her on it. Her natural precocity will take over from there. But it don't make them run faster. It makes them run as fast as they can for a longer period of time. There's a difference, if that makes sense to you. It is just a matter of staying out of the way of Mother Nature from there."

"Mother Nature?"

"Yup. It's a common mistake to over train them, to think you know more about them than Mother Nature does."

"Does Mother Nature talk to you?"

"You think I'm crazy, and I may be. It ain't like hearing voices. That horse talks to you if you'll just listen. It'll tell you when it's happy or when it's scared or when it's hurt. It will tell you when you are riding it too much or not enough, when you are going too fast or too slow, or when you're riding her too hard. It will tell you what it can do and how it can do it. It is telling you everything you need to know if you just know how to listen. It talks to you the same way your own body talks to you. It is talking. It will tell you when it is ready to run fast, to break wind over the racetrack. The question isn't whether she's talking. The question is are you listening?"

"You gotta be a horse listener."

"That would be about right. A horse listener rather than a horse whisperer."

"You give the other horses besides the filly poison ivy?"

"Nope. Them nags?" I laughed, sweeping my hand dismissively across shed row where most of the horses either hung their necks over the stall doors or nibbled at the paint on the stall doors, the picture of lethargy. "The only thing that's saving them is they tell me we can't beat them anymore. They are pathetic. They refuse to run. You know. They really can't outrun their pedigrees. They literally throw themselves on the ground and refuse to run at all. They quit. To tell you the truth, I can't bear to even look at them, no less clean their stalls, pay to ship them, pay to feed them, carry fresh hay and water to them. Lizzie W is different. She's the only racehorse in this barn. The question is going to be whether she's a champion."

Of course, I was right about Lizzie W. I implored Mr. Tripps to take an interest in her progress. He refused. He even dismissed the notion that the help, as he put it, should feel entitled to initiate any correspondence whatsoever with a gentleman of his pedigree. Yet something very troubling happened when we got the filly to Saratoga.

***

On race day, everybody said our opponent in the match race, the champion colt Captain Moore, was unbeatable. He sure looked it. The bay colt was twice the size of our filly, and the colt was on the muscle, a pure specimen.

Captain Moore's coat was brushed to brilliance, and his tail was braided, like it was groomed for the photographer in the winner's circle. The horse's past performances sustained that opinion, too. The colt was undefeated. It had won his last race by open lengths. Captain Moore had distinguished itself over the prestigious courses in Kentucky, Texas, and Louisiana against the finest horses in the nation, and he had done so with authority. Now, its connections were taking on the four day meet at the Saratoga trotting course.

I rose early on race day. The grey light of dawn had just begun to rim the horizon, and the air was cool and the grass was still wet. The sky was high and deep and all around. There wasn't a trace of rain or a single cloud head in the sky, which was unusual for Saratoga. By race time, the trotting course was definitely going to be fast.

I believe a different man, a stranger, emerged out of Mr. Tripps that day as well, a greedy man, an evil man, a conniving man, a man to match the Evil Man growing inside of me. I predicted Mr. Tripps was the type of man who would bask in the glory of the victory, assuming there was any realistic possibility of victory that day. Thoughts of the evil side of Mr. Tripps invaded my mind as I walked the filly over to the trotting grounds. Henry carried a bucket of water in one hand, a towel slung over his shoulder, and a flask of whiskey in his right hand. While I yanked the brass shank to keep the filly's mind on her business, Henry threw up the flask and felt the burn of whiskey all the way down to his guts.

"Put that away, Henry," I cautioned. "I don't want the filly to smell the odor. I can't take any chances on her freaking out. It's bad enough that we have never seen how she'll react to attention of the audience she's going to get in the paddock."

An audience of more than one thousand people had descended upon the trotting grounds that day. They had come from all over to witness what the newspapers were calling the grand spectacle of the inaugural Saratoga meeting. Every element of society was represented on the procession over the muddy ruts, breaks, and crevices of Union Avenue on the way to the trotting grounds. The flow of traffic seemed endless.

Some came by finely upholstered buggies and carriages; others came by rough-hewn flatbed wagons; and still others came on horseback or on foot, but they all came.

They came from the gambling houses and the mineral baths. Some suspended riotous parties, taking a break from the opulence of linen table cloths, fine crystal, and hanging chandeliers at the Congress Hotel just long enough to join the procession. There were counts and countesses, dukes and duchesses, and princes and princesses from far away kingdoms; colored help newly arrived from the South; bankers and accountants and lawyers and their gossipy wives; young men wearing black waistcoats eager to compete for the hand of one of the countless debutantes; and debutantes fresh from boarding schools with an appetite for the attention of suitable male companionship. This patch work of the fabric of society had only one thing that united it all: They were drawn to the inherent excitement and spectacle of a thoroughbred match race, like moths to a flame. It would have been little more than classic understatement to say we were nervous. We were flat-out scared to death.

What if the filly was not up to the challenge? It was a match race, but most of the elements of luck had been removed by the race conditions written by John Morrissey, the visionary who owned the trotting course and believed thoroughbred racing would attract crowds to Saratoga. Mr. Morrissey had formed a partnership of like-minded gentlemen to support his vision.

The match race in the four day meet, the first of its kind at Saratoga, was intended to showcase the excitement and spectacle of thoroughbred racing and the wisdom of Mr. Morrissey's vision. He was betting his money on the proposition that one day Saratoga could attract crowds for things other than the mineral baths, the casinos, and the wild parties. That thing was the majestic beauty of thoroughbreds competing for money. The match race would be run in three heats, so the filly would need to beat Captain Moore at least twice that day in order to win, an unlikelihood of epic proportion.

The paddock was occupied by men wearing black suits and stove pipe hats. The sun burned down upon the filly. I hurriedly tacked her up, careful to smooth out all of the wrinkles on the saddle cloth. Even a single wrinkle on that blanket over the withers would make even a professional horse like Lizzie W act up.

The Horse

I threw the tiny saddle over her back. I yanked the girth band under her belly. I tied the whole affair off with a stern loop and a second yank. As I looked over her back to adjust the saddle, I caught a glimpse of Captain Moore across the paddock. He was massive and tucked up. There were bands of rippling muscle everywhere that were unmistakable and announced the prospect of unprecedented fitness, brutal power, and absolute speed. Our little filly would not only have to beat a boy, she would have to beat a big boy at that.

The colt was on the muscle. Its eyes bulged as if its life depended on the outcome of the race. It snorted as it bowed its neck and stared at the ground, like a bull readying itself to charge at absolutely anything that moved, including our little filly.

Mr. Tripps calmly walked over to us wearing a crisp Victorian dinner jacket, a fresh haircut and shave, the finest vest sold in Boston or New York, and the smell of his expensive Hour d'et Homme on the air. Mr. Morrissey, who had funded the purse with his own money, was with him. This was the first time I got within earshot of John Morrissey.

The most flattering way to describe John Morrissey's reputation was to simply call him a vicious man and to leave it at that. It was best to leave the details to conjecture. Standing with feet spread apart authoritatively in an expensive tailored suit with sleeves that stopped short of his wrists due to the bulging muscle groups across his chest, across his back, and on his arms, John Morrissey's nervous demeanor made him always seem as though he was more than a few pews shy of the altar of respectability, perhaps a wanted man who needed to remain aware of his surroundings to avoid arrest.

He was a career criminal, gambler, and heavyweight bare-knuckles boxing champion who once beat a man named "Yankee Sullivan" senseless in a title bout that lasted 37 rounds before an outdoor audience in Boston of three thousand blood thirsty fans. The historical record notes that John Morrissey bit, pounded, and gouged "Yankee Sullivan" in each one of those 37 rounds. John Morrissey later boasted that he had used any means at his disposal to prevail and the rules were only momentary inconveniences. Nothing stood in the way of the ferocity of his ambition. He accepted other prize fights in California, Ontario, and Troy, New York to similar results. He conducted his business affairs at the Saratoga trotting course in much the same manner that he treated his opponents in the boxing ring.

His shoulders stood out the same way granite building blocks stand out alongside the majestic

The Horse

columns on the steps of the grand courthouses in New York and Philadelphia. I am not sure how he earned the nickname "Old Smoke," but it might have had something to do with his black bushy beard, black peasant eyes, and slick black hair. It also might have harkened back to his impoverished Irish childhood and his lust to overcome his roots as an Irish immigrant in America by any means necessary, whether those means included working on the docks, hanging wall paper, joining a gang, throwing his bare knuckles, or by setting apartments on fire as a tactic to compel delinquent tenants to surrender possession of their abodes without a legal challenge. In a peculiar way, criminality aside, he was uniquely American.

There was an aggressive confidence about him that matched his cruel jaw line. He had immense hands, the kind of hands capable of throwing around bales of hay, convincing wayward cattle to comply with his demands, dominating unlucky opponents in a boxing ring or dispatching practically anything else that got in his way. He was the type of man who looked more likely to throw a straight right hand in a prize fight or to hang around in the shadows of darkened alleys lying in wait for his next victim rather than negotiating the polite and subtle nuances of the high society of the horse racing set. Indeed, in real life he fancied placing large wagers on himself, and when he won, and he always won, he smiled broadly and was more than capable of collecting gambling proceeds from those unfortunate souls who were reluctant to make good on their promises to pay what they owed, whether their moment of truth came in a saloon, an alley, a church, or in the poor fellow's bedroom. It always came at the hands of John Morrissey, and it didn't matter to him where or how he collected his cash. It only mattered that he collected.

The gambling proceeds enriched him to the point where he could afford to finance an impressive string of casinos and gambling houses and to purchase the fine tailored suits he wore to Saratoga in the summer of 1863. The elegance of his suits did absolutely nothing to hide the truth evidenced by the angry scar tissue that had formed over his right eyebrow courtesy of a gash delivered by a knowledgeable boxing opponent who once succeeded in smuggling a cake of plaster into the ring he managed to conceal beneath the fancy waistband of his boxing togs. He wanted to beat John Morrissey at his own game. Of course, it didn't work. John Morrissey beat the hell out of the man after the gash sent blood trailing down his face.

These experiences turned John Morrissey into a serious man who rarely smiled. Through enterprise and arrogance, this man was inspired to buy the Saratoga trotting course. So, John Morrissey and his partners, William R. Travers, John R. Hunter, and Leonard Jerome, who likely were used as Morrissey's alter egos, were the visionaries who dreamed of turning Saratoga into the thoroughbred racing capital of the world. In short, Morrissey convinced the titans of the thoroughbred industry to not only attend parties thrown in Saratoga for people who enjoy being rich together or simply lounging about in the healing properties of the waters of Saratoga's famous spas and baths, but to ship their strings North to race horses there. He was gambling on the inherent beauty, dignity and speed of the racehorse to attract large crowds of well-heeled spectators to the excitement of match races. The plan was beginning to work.

"I have a nice place here," Morrissey said, his eyes nervously darting between the filly in the paddock, the crowd of reporters that had formed, and certain bookies in the crowd who accepted large wagers, including a wager staked on our filly by Mr. Morrissey himself. In this fashion, he had managed to make money even at a time while the Civil War continued to rage in different pockets of the nation. Although the $2,700 purse for the match race came out of Mr. Morrissey's pocket, he easily recovered that sum and more through the dollar admission fee charged to the thousands of patrons.

"This is blatantly disrespectful," Mr. Tripps insisted.

"What?" Mr. Morrissey responded.

"The bettors are dismissing the chances of my filly at odds of over 100 to 1."

"Don't take it personally."

"Don't take it personally!"

"Correct."

"Dismissing my filly at those shocking odds is the same as dismissing me personally, isn't it? It is shorthand, isn't it? A serious man brings a serious horse to the races. This absolutely is shorthand. The bettors are not only saying they do not believe in my horse. In saying so, it necessarily follows that they do not believe in me. Do they think I would lead a horse over here that is not a capable animal, not capable of competing against the likes of Captain Moore?"

"You give a one-eyed jockey going by the name of Sewell the mount on your little filly, a boy capable of seeing only half of the course on a sunny day and probably less than half of the race itself, and you wonder why at least half of the folks are dismissing the betting proposition," he laughed. "I mean, it's enough of a disadvantage to race a filly against a colt and at equal weights. And if that wasn't enough of a handicap, you think to put a jockey up with only one eye! Sure, you'll have three legs of the match race to prove them all wrong, but you have to admit Captain Moore is a magnificent looking animal, isn't he?"

"That boy may have only one eye, but boy he can ride better than a jockey with three eyes. Besides, looks like a lot more than half of the bettors are dismissing us."

"I said at least half."

"And Captain Moore is a magnificent looking animal, but can he run?"

"Oh, he can run alright, but I am staking a small wager on your little filly anyway. That's where the smart money is, on your animal. There is public money on Captain Moore, but the smart inside money is on your filly."

"I certainly hope so."

The two men only registered parenthetical interest in the filly while they chatted, like their wealth alone was more than enough to make them immune to nervous excitement or any other of the lesser traits that bedeviled members of the lower classes of society. I secretly longed for inclusion in the society of Charles Ogden Tripps and John Morrissey. I admired it. In their world, men owned strings of racehorses, trained them out of their own stables, and lived in fine homes surrounded by rolling grounds. These men were truly free.

I smoked cigars and wore high collar shirts to fit in, but it didn't work. My cigars were cheap. Mr. Tripps smoked expensive imports. The blue smoke of his cigars smelled full and sweet. The grey smoke of my cigars smelled like burnt paper. However, no matter what I smoked or wore, I couldn't deny the Evil Man that was growing inside.

If Mr. Tripps hadn't made it clear in his demeanor, in the way he asked me questions without expecting an answer, the way he looked past me toward the horizon as if I was invisible, and in the code he held sacred between the gentlemen of his class, if the courts, schools, legislatures, even the prosecution of the Civil War itself didn't appear designed to exclude members of my class from ever joining their world, I might have been able to deny the existence of the Evil Man growing inside. I was a logical man. I wanted to deny the Evil Man.

The importance of the occasion at hand did nothing to discourage this affect. Neither Mr. Tripps nor Mr. Morrissey said a word to me or Henry, not a note of greeting or congratulations, not a query, not a concern, nothing. It was as though we were both invisible attending to the filly in the Saratoga paddock.

The Horse

As soon as the boy who wore our stable's scarlet satin jersey with white blocks, white britches, matching scarlet satin cap, and black riding boots, a boy who was blacker than a burnt-out prairie at sunset, reported to the filly's side, I gave him instructions on how to ride the race, cupped the heel of his boot in one hand, and threw him up on Lizzie W's back. He swung his right leg over the horse, grabbed the reins, and found each iron with the toe of each of his boots, and our filly began to dance on her toes. He stood and adjusted the irons before returning his backsides to the saddle. The horses walked out of the paddock in tandem and out to the trotting course to announce their presence to the crowd that pressed ever closer to the rail. The horses broke off and galloped out to warm up over the evenly groomed course.

The first leg of the race was a sprint. There was no grandstand. However, thralls of fashionably dressed men and women crowded the rail. Their faces were barely visible under gay umbrellas, black stove pipe hats, and straw boaters with brightly colored hat bands.

Both horses worked up a lather during the warmup gallop, so their coats grew slick and black in color. The starters drew a single rope across the course to ensure the horses got off to a level and fair start. The starter held up a red flag. The horses danced. The horses gathered together to face the rope. The starter yanked down the flag. The boys dropped the rope, and the race was on.

The horses galloped as a pair, rating over the first quarter of the race to the near turn of the oval. The excitement in the crowd was palpable. Both boys stood up in the irons, like mirror images. The horses matched strides, picking up the pace along the backstretch. There still was no separation.

The horses kicked their knees high and their necks were outstretched. There was no sign of fatigue in either horse. The boys began to urge the horses to pick up the pace around the far turn by pumping their legs and pushing the irons, but each boy was still standing up.

As they turned for home, the horses quickened and dueled under heavy urging. Both boys bounced furiously in the saddle, pushed their mount's neck forward from behind the ears, and made liberal use of their sticks, furiously whipping and slashing horse flesh, asking for one final burst of speed to the finish line. That's when the crowd roared. There were random vulgarities and exhortations hurled from the masses as well, as if commentary could assert some sort of magical, extrasensory influence over the outcome of the race.

Captain Moore responded to his boy's slashing whip first and began to pull away. The filly tried

The Horse

to respond, but she was green and seemed to have problems coordinating her strides, untangling her legs, keeping her head straight on forward, and unleashing a closing kick of any consequence. The seasoned Captain Moore had no such problem. He beat the filly to the line. The colt had taken the first heat of the match race by slightly over two lengths.

"Bloody ridiculous!" Mr. Tripps screamed, massively enraged.

He slammed his program to the ground. His eyes darted around the crowd to see if anyone had witnessed the outburst. Emotion was simply never put on display in society by a gentleman. It was one of the many unwritten rules of society.

Back in the paddock, Sewell slid belly down off of Lizzie W's back and landed gently on his toes. Henry settled the horse at the bridle using both hands to hold the shank. I used a wet towel to wipe the filly's face. Her ribs were still heaving from exhaustion. I overturned a bucket of water on the top of her head. The water rolled down her face. Her tongue licked at the water. That's when I suspected she was not the worse for wear. She wanted to drink water. However, I didn't let her drink or graze. I didn't want anything in her system that she might vomit up during the second heat of the race, which was only twenty minutes away. I wanted to avoid the risk the filly might swallow her tongue, bleed from the lungs, or vomit during the second leg of the race.

I felt Lizzie W's ankles. There was no heat, a good sign. I squeezed her canon bones. She didn't flinch. The filly was none the worse for wear. She was dead fit to run the second leg. We had hope.

I used the towel to rub her face, neck, and shoulders. I lifted her tail and wiped away the lather that had formed between her hind legs. The filly had given all she had. I wasn't disappointed with her effort. I wanted her to know how proud I was of her gallantry. There was no failure. There was only triumph over that course. The only way to fail at a trial is to fail to try.

This filly had tried. She had given all she had. She acquitted herself nicely according to that universal standard of competition. It didn't matter how much money her backers had gambled and lost with the bookies.

I kissed her forehead and smelled her rubbery lips. She tossed her head to signal how much she appreciated the conciliatory nature of the tender touch. Mr. Tripps, on the other hand, would have nothing to do with the idea of defeat. He was a man who only found relevance at the bottom line, and the bottom line of the first heat was the filly lost.

The Horse

Mr. Tripps knew a loser when he saw one, and the filly was a loser, at least in his eyes. Therefore, Mr. Tripps turned his back on the paddock and stepped into a group of men. The group engulfed him. His trail of blue cigar smoke was all that was visible of him from our vantage point in the paddock. I imagined that he had distanced himself from the outcome with a string of dismissive vulgarities.

The second heat proceeded identically to the first. The horses galloped eagerly across the course and into the near turn. There were screams and shouts of encouragement from the thousands gathered at the rail.

Captain Moore set the pace along the picturesque Saratoga backstretch. The boy on our filly changed tactics, wrapping the reins more tightly in his fist, whispering to the filly's ear through the wind, and taking back in second. The filly got the idea. She slowed, settled, and stalked the pace. Captain Moore remained muscular and eager on the lead.

The colt galloped with his full force into the wind, and the lead got even wider. The dirt on the course kicked back and flew into the air behind Captain Moore's powerful hind legs. There were several lengths of daylight between the colt on the lead and the filly stalking in second. Indeed, the colt was a threat to run away with the race, particularly if the filly did not respond soon.

The colt held plenty of energy in reserve into the far turn. Our boy's tactic wasn't working. Captain Moore was not weakening at all. Instead, he lost contact with the filly. He was easily five lengths in front. The only issue was whether the colt would finish powerfully or lose energy and stop at the crucial last stages of the race.

The boy slapped the filly with the stick. She picked up the pace around the far turn. She started to close furiously on her right lead. The horses swung around the turn with the filly gaining ground fast. The boy pulled the reins with his right hand making the filly swing very wide outside of the colt's path at the rail. When the boy sat down on the saddle and challenged the filly to run on her left lead by slashing her left shoulder with the stick, she exploded into an all-out gallop.

She rushed to the lead and drew alongside the colt and then ran past a tiring Captain Moore in a single prodigious breath, like a stiff wind whipping across the course. The raw brutality of the move nearly made the filly stagger off her shoes, until she recovered, straightened out toward the finish line, and unleashed fluid strides yearning for the finish line. Conversely, the colt was beginning to bog down and tire.

The Horse

The filly didn't show any signs of tiring. The boy put the whip in his teeth and switched it to his right hand. He slapped the filly on the shoulder with the crop and then beat her right hip repeatedly. She switched leads again and ran off to the finish line. It was a resounding four length victory. The second heat belonged to Lizzie W. This deadlocked the match race at one heat apiece. The rubber leg of the match race was next.

The filly was greeted by applause in the paddock. I pulled off her linen tongue tie. There was blood. I pulled back her rubbery lips exposing the immensity of her dentures. I pulled against the bit. The filly responded by fully opening her mouth. I looked at her long, coarse tongue. If she bled from the lungs, or swallowed her tongue, she was at risk of suffocation. As I examined her, Mr. Tripps pushed forward out of the crowd. Suddenly, he showed interest in claiming the filly's achievement.

He patted her hip and walked around to where I was working on the horse. The smell of his Hour d'et Homme was so strong it made the filly show the wild white of her eyes and shy away. She reared, throwing her front legs into the air. I calmly gave her more than enough tolerance on the shank so she could thrash freely and return all four feet safely to earth. If I made the mistake of yanking the shank to make her behave, the filly might flip and land on her back. That wouldn't have done much for her disposition prior to the decisive third leg of the match race.

On cue, Lizzie W landed gently, but the white of her eyes still showed. She snorted and complained. I asked Mr. Tripps to return to the crowd and spare the filly any more agitation. I knew she objected to the smell of his perfume and told him so.

The third heat saw Captain Moore go off as the prohibitive favorite with the bookies. The idea that the powerful colt would avenge the only loss on his record had gained considerable backing. The break was clean.

Remarkably, Captain Moore elected to go to the lead yet again, and yet again, Sewell, the one-eyed jockey on our filly, took back. The filly tracked the colt all the way around the oval. The silhouette of the battle raging against the rolling green hills of Saratoga was a thing of beauty. The filly was content to sit slightly off the pace. When they turned for home, the filly swung wide and galloped past the colt. The muscular colt was tiring yet again.

A roar went up from the crowd. A few people began to hoot and holler, like dogs let off of the chain. Others ran up to the rail to get a better look at the spectacle, like nothing else at all matter in the world.

The Horse

The colt climbed and yearned for more run to keep up, but he had nothing left. By contrast, Lizzie W was full of run. She galloped clear to the line for an open length victory. The mighty colt, Captain Moore, had lost. Lizzie W, a filly, had become the champion of Saratoga!

****

By the time Lizzie W returned from the gallop out, the winner's circle was busy with admirers. A retinue of news reporters with notebooks swarmed the victorious and glowing Mr. Tripps, like he was some sort of celebrity. Henry hooked the shank on the bridle and settled the horse. The boy took off his hat to pose for the photograph. The photographer already had his camera tripod set up. He disappeared under the contraption's black hood. There was a camera flash and a wisp of smoke.

The boy slid off the back of the horse, unhooked the girth band, and pulled off the saddle. That's when I overheard Mr. Tripps confide to a reporter from the *Ballston Spa Courier* that he had already stolen my interest in Lizzie W and sold her off to an outfit in Lexington where she would become a broodmare.

I was overcome with rage. He expanded his answer by telling the reporter in so many words that he had made my share of the horse vanish by manipulating the foal papers and the bill of sale. Then, he had the audacity to look at me, or should I say he had the audacity to look through me, as though I was a perfect stranger.

I had come to hate Mr. Tripps from that moment, you see. My mind went blank. I saw revenge as my only option. Mr. Tripps had unleashed the other man that is inside of all of us, the stranger, the Evil Man, the man who is conniving, the man who covets revenge. It was that level of revenge, spite, anger that led me to rob the filly of the naked glory of a champion at full gallop over the proving grounds of a racetrack. In some respects, I had robbed us all of the chance to observe the simple greatness of the horse, perhaps from a distance, perhaps at the end of a wager, or perhaps as a congregant at the altar of Mother Nature, the precious opportunity to witness the clash of indomitable will against crass mediocrity, the poetry of open strides through open air against the poverty of human opinion, and to behold those things in the context of a thoroughbred horse race. I had traded the glory of extraordinary achievement for rage, and there was a steep price to pay for the arrogance of the Evil Man. I knew my fate. Mr. Tripps's interview in the winner's circle that day changed me. I surrendered my life to the Evil Man that day.

God is not tempted by evil. God brings every evil deed, every secret thing, to judgment. Mr. Tripps had unleashed the Evil Man, and the Evil Man only cared about simple urges and evil deeds, like revenge. If you wish to appreciate fully what went on in the mind of this conniving man, the one who committed this horrible crime, I would say it all started when I was a boy back on the farm, and I can even pinpoint the exact day it began to blossom. Thinking back, the only way to begin to expose the Evil Man is by going back to how the story began while I was still a boy working on horse farms in Louisiana, Texas, and Kentucky.

****

"Hol own, boy. Ah gotta catch muh breath," my father drawled, pausing from the work of filing the horse's hoof perched on his thigh under his blacksmith's apron. We were on shed row of Alexander Hancock's farm in Lexington, Kentucky at the time. This is a part of my history I regret betraying even more bitterly than the crime of destroying Lizzie W for reasons this confession will soon reveal.

My father, who was known affectionately as "Shoeboy," resumed the work of filing the hoof of one of Mr. Hancock's prized geldings. He didn't look away from the work while he spoke, "Yuh gotta gift, boy,' he said over the metallic rasping sound made by the file. "It's a gift to know the secrets of horses. It's a rare gift. Yuh gotta remember that. Yuh gotta remember to use your gift wisely."

He spat a stream of brown tobacco juice at the floor and paused to admire the shape of the hoof. He looked at the barn floor and squinted as if he was trying to figure out something else to say. He said nothing and returned reluctantly to the work of filing, like he had wanted to say something else, but decided against it. Instead of expanding his advice, he spat at the floor again and just kept filing.

The sound of my father filing that hoof would later haunt me at Saratoga, and it haunts me in this hotel room today. My father could have counseled me on the tricks of horse trading and how to protect oneself against predatory business practices. He could have shown me the many ways a gift like mine could be stolen by deception. Yet, he chose to say nothing.

Thinking back, this omission allowed a different man to grow inside of me, the stranger, the Evil Man, the conniving man, the bitter man, the man who covets revenge, the man capable of horrific deeds, the man capable of killing Lizzie W, and this stranger, this monster, was easily vexed toward violence.

The gift I was born with showed me how to flat-out ride. I could ride horses hard, ride them sideways, coax them, ride them anyway they needed to be ridden, really get them to go, and I could train them even better than I could ride them. I could train them hard. I could train them easy. It didn't matter. I could teach them to absolutely break wind on a racetrack, run their eyeballs out. I could train the meanness into them, so they were not content to merely run alongside other horses in a herd, but to really get after it, pick up their feet, and breeze straight past any field. I could give a boy a leg up and watch that jockey float over a stretch of ground so fast it gave the other jockeys wind burn. However, as I've said, aside from those feats of horsemanship, my father never taught me the secrets of money or horse trading or any of the finer points that are important in society. I was at a decided disadvantage in dealing with the likes of Mr. Tripps. If you wish to call me a hick, so be it.

Yet the Evil Man was far from slow. On the contrary, he saw many of the things other people overlooked. For example, he knew the moniker "Shoeboy" wasn't a term of endearment or a testament to my father's skill as a blacksmith, like an extra gold chevron on the uniform of a Confederate officer. It was actually a form of racial insult. The stranger delighted in seeking revenge for slights like this. In many ways, while my father was filing down the hoof he had perched on his thigh under his blacksmith's apron with the weight of the entire beast suspended over his right shoulder, the evil that would eventually destroy the filly at Saratoga had already begun to grow inside of me. Many are likely to look at that evil categorically as simply the machinations of a criminal mind. I prefer to call it a vulnerability.

Mr. Charles Ogden Tripps, Charlie, could simply have kept his word and honored our agreement, and the filly would still be alive. However, instead of keeping his word, he elected to steal my stake in the filly by outright, and shameless, acts of deception. He reneged on our agreement to sell the filly on the open market after the race and split the proceeds of the sale according to the terms of our partnership agreement.

"Don't you go forgetting to use that gift wisely boy, hear?" I still remember that stream of brown tobacco juice my father spat at the floor, the way he admired the hoof to measure the work left to be done, and how he simply kept filing, offering no further guidance. The sound of that file against that hoof at the hands of that man still haunts my sleep.

My father was a man who let his work do his talking, and he would never have approved of the version of me that sought revenge. However, work, alone, isn't particularly good at telling the truth, and the truth, told poorly, is a lie. That lie is a part of my father's legacy. I'd love to say he was a blacksmith on one of the prestigious farms in Louisiana, Texas, and Kentucky his entire life, but that wouldn't be entirely true.

I grew up kicking around horse farms in upstate New York, the kind of farms with dilapidated barns the wind has little difficulty disrespecting due to missing doors or gaps between clapboards. But the inherent poverty of my childhood didn't interfere with the God-given privilege of understanding the subtle intricacies of a horse, like the secrets underlying the mystery of its flesh. My father taught me the trick to making horses submit to the will of a human hand, even the ornery types. They all learned to stand while he filed away at their hooves, measured their shoes, fired the shoes, and proceeded to shod them by pounding nails through the shoes onto hoof after hoof quickly and expertly. I never dreamed a horse, once dead, could rise from the dead to return to life as a ghost, but I would eventually learn otherwise. I tossed all of this history away, every bit of it, including cherished values, to commit a horrible crime against Lizzie W. In doing so, I reduced myself from a member of one of the subordinate classes Mr. Tripps abhorred to the rank of a common criminal.

*****

I suppose the reporters from the *Ballston Journal* and the *Daily Saratogonia* secretly felt entitled to interview me for a story about how a lowly horse trainer made it to the winner's circle alongside a gentleman of the caliber of Mr. Tripps, particularly on that joyous occasion. I declined to answer any of their questions. I was convinced that my story was a private matter, and private matters simply are not laid bare in plain view in society, particularly not in the wake of the historic victory of our filly over the legendary Captain Moore on the Saratoga trotting course, a stunning result achieved before the eyes of all members of society. Nevertheless, nothing could stop Mr. Tripps from basking in the attention of the reporters, and his responses to pointed questions swiftly became news wired to Europe and the rest of the civilized world.

In this instance, strict composure is absolutely required of the upper ranks of society, the privileged few with the means to summer in Saratoga in the middle of a civil war, the gentlemen who announce their membership in the privileged classes in ways foreign to me, like the way they hold a crystal flute to sip champagne at dinner or pause before addressing a member of the wait staff or dismiss an interruption by showing no emotion while not bothering to break the cadence of a frank conversation spoken in a mysterious code or really any one of the thousands of other permutations of society held sacred between them, and the ladies who do not perspire or partake of any of the darker emotions, preferring instead to wear the finest hats and linens while fluttering like powdered moths at the elbows of delicate gentlemen possessed of inherited money. The Saratoga winner's circle is a place where people aspire to gather to enjoy the full weight of exclusive privilege together. It certainly wasn't an appropriate place and time to trigger a scandal that attends a dispute over money. I didn't care. I sensed betrayal.

"What are your plans for the filly?" The question was directed at Mr. Tripps from deep inside the pack of reporters.

"I sold her off already. She's getting shipped to a prestigious farm in the South. She'll be covered by one of the top sires," Mr. Tripps gloated. "She'll make a promising broodmare, don't you think?"

"And cut me out of my end of the filly, which is exactly fifty percent of that horse, an interest that is equal to your interest, making us equal partners?" I said, interrupting Mr. Tripps's repartee with the reporters.

Mr. Tripps tossed his head. Instead of showing emotion, he simply ignored my plea and continued to speak to the reporters. There was something about the word *equal* that struck Mr. Tripps as vulgar. It was a word that meant the speaker quite possibly might never understand the secret codes that govern society. The word has absolutely no thoughtful meaning. Words like money and power and negotiation were the operative words in Mr. Tripps's world. Equality was a word that meant absolutely nothing to him.

I hated the dismissive way Mr. Tripps ignored me. It was only when one of the reporters looked startled and stopped taking notes that Mr. Tripps even bothered to address me parenthetically. "There will be no discussion of your end," he scoffed.

I told him I was holding on to my interest in the filly. He could ignore me if he liked, but there would be no sale until I approved of the asking price, and this would be over a period of time when all suitors were given a chance to weigh in on the proposition. I announced my intention to measure the filly's value

The Horse

on the open market, and I would take every cent of my fifty percent split.

The reporters began to scribble furiously. "The matter of ownership in the filly is not open to debate. It is a thing decided," he confided.

There is something every horseman knows. The sole *indicia* of ownership are papers, foal papers. Those papers must be on file with the Jockey Club. Therefore, true ownership in any racehorse is never seriously a matter in dispute, unless there is a bill of sale. It is not controversial. And if a cloud forms over the title, there are courts everywhere with the jurisdiction to settle such matters, and they are paid handsomely for the service. Filing a lawsuit to settle the issue is not too much to ask, is it? Whether it is too much to ask or not is not important. While everyone is free to register a grievance in a court of law, the word free carries a different ring when it pertains to litigation against the powerful. It is presumptuous and foolhardy to suggest otherwise. That was the very word Mr. Tripps used to describe my rights.

"Everyone is free to appeal to a court of law, and that freedom extends to you as well," he mocked.

The way Mr. Tripps used the word *free* carried a distinctive sting, a different weight, a different angle, like he knew the word was loaded. I knew there was never a realistic chance that a lowly horse trainer could prevail in court against a man as powerful as Mr. Tripps.

Do you see my situation? Do you see the "spot" Mr. Tripps had me in? Do you see the "spot" society had me in? Could I count on a court anywhere to rule justly in my favor? No? This "spot" will make all of the other aspects of this confession clear.

In the early fall of that year – eight days before the new connections were scheduled to appear at our barn in Saratoga to claim ownership of the filly, to lead her straight off the grounds and out of our lives forever, I began to convince Henry that we needed to show these folks, including Mr. Tripps himself, that revenge is a commodity that is available *equally* to the members of all social classes, and the idea of mortality can swiftly and breathlessly become much more than merely a friend of revenge. It can become revenge's most reliable romantic partner. I told Henry we needed a plan: I reminded him of the trouble a colored groom who had impregnated an underaged white girl could expect from the local authorities, and the fight required to repel the attack of a lynch mob, and that any peace he enjoyed in life could be made to vanish with the snap of a judge's slender fingers or the drop of a noose over his head after it had been thrown over a tree branch. Conversely, if he helped me, and we succeeded

The Horse

in hiding its flesh while it rotted, his indiscretion with the girl would vanish along with it.

"What do you need me to do?" he asked after I made my pitch.

I regretted blackmailing Henry in this way. I really did. However, I was out of options. I was in a "spot," and Henry had the misfortune of knowing all of the details. If I made the filly vanish, the first person the authorities would question would be Henry, and Henry would be the first person to give the authorities enough evidence to convict me. Now, if Henry was an accomplice, it would remove his incentive to cooperate with the authorities. On the contrary, he would have every incentive to avoid attention and to lie outright.

"I regret this is even necessary. I love that horse," I said.

"Why did Mr. Tripps do this to you?"

"Greed is a poisonous drug."

The Evil Man inside already had a remedy for Mr. Tripps. I had even worked out a plan. The only question is when I would decide to share it with Henry. I would swing into the filly's stall and execute her.

The horse can be tied off in the confined space inside of her stall. The barn is abandoned overnight. The other operations rely on barking dogs to signal there is a stir in the barn at night. I would walk the dogs off the grounds before getting the attack underway. I knew the horse would scream and thrash about wildly and rail against her own mortality with a wild fight. It was an attribute of her regal bloodlines.

I would end the filly's life with a gunshot. Championship caliber race horses have far too much life, too much fight, to accept the idea of defeat or the inevitability of death quietly. In order to make it clean, a racehorse must be shot, preferably through the skull. Then, the body swiftly bloats and the limbs stiffen with gangrene, and the transformation is almost comical in its quickness. An athletic, supple animal with limber extremities that shoot skyward with gangrene, and the mucous and pink entrails oozing out of every possible orifice, like the rectum, the mouth, the ears, and the vaginal canal. Those pinkish entrails can be counted on to stink immediately, and the stench attracts swarms of insects. Worse yet, the stench attracts human attention. The work of dispatching a one thousand pound animal to a shallow grave to hide all evidence of the crime and to do so quickly was not a job for one man. It was a job for two. That's why I needed Henry.

Otherwise, the deed would hardly be kept secret from the locals very long. Word of it could be counted on to reach the federal marshals who prowled everywhere due to the prosecution of the Civil War.

The Horse

The horse would need to be covered on the exact spot where she went over after the gunshot, and the body would need to be covered under the haymow to tamp down the smell of the occasion.

I told Henry to think of the ignominy of a penniless life without ever tasting the simple satisfaction of revenge. I was aware that Henry quite possibly drew the analogy between this ambition and the murderous intentions of jilted lovers who discover the infidelity of romantic partners first hand, by walking in on them, by witnessing them in the midst of the act itself.

"If this doesn't suit you," I said, "you might take your chances with the country bumpkins, the trees in the woods, the dogs, the marshals, and the bounty hunters."

Henry was far from calm. He was nervous, even desperate. The girl was already quite obviously far along in her pregnancy. If she confided that the real father was a colored groom, Henry would be hunted as a fugitive. If the newborn turns out to be of mixed race, this would remove the element of intrigue and replace it with the element of scandal, but Henry was a man who had impregnated a mere girl. This is a felony. Do you see the "spot" Henry was in?

"I wonder if it will be painful to the filly," Henry whimpered.

"It will be quick," I said, as if the speed of the endeavor was any consolation.

Like a dead horse's extremities, the plan had already begun to calcify in my mind. It was irrevocable, a thing decided.

****

I led Henry down shed row. There were plenty of empty stalls at the end of the barn. Most of the horses had already been shipped to the South for the winter.

I pointed to the last empty stall and told Henry we would need to muck it out, make a clean dirt floor, and dig a trench at least two feet deep. I figured that would be deep enough to do the job. I told Henry we would need to work quickly. I explained that the biological processes that follow a slaughter would make the filly begin to stink almost immediately. We would also need to get the job done without leaving a single trace of the crime. That's when Henry's hands began to tremble.

He uncorked a silver flask and threw it up. He closed his eyes as the whiskey backed up in the neck of the flask and gurgled against his lips. The delicate chain attached to the cork made a scratching noise at the side of the flask.

Later that morning, a coach and four horses unexpectedly came rushing up to the barn in a determined gallop that sent the dogs barking and snarling and turning themselves inside out. The coachman didn't dare confront the dogs. Instead, he waited up on the coach's box for us to present ourselves from the shadows of the barn. It wasn't until we had succeeded in quieting the dogs that the coachman descended.

He addressed me formally, "Mr. Holmes?"

"Yes, I am he," I replied.

The coachman produced a court order embossed with a red wax seal. He handed the paper to me. "Good day," he said curtly and walked away.

The fellow climbed up the coach to regain his spot on the box, shook the reins at the horses, and left in a cloud of dust.

"This is a cease and desist order issued by a court of law out of Albany," I said, examining the contents of the papers.

I calmly folded the papers and tucked them away in my pocket. I made sustained eye contact with Henry. We knew what was required of us.

****

On summer nights that are pleasantly orange and unmolested by angry clouds, the dance of fire flies appears in the new air over Saratoga. How do they know to wait for the sunlight to give way to darkness to begin the dance? Later, after the air cools, the fire flies no longer light. Instead, the noise of crickets and the moan of frogs take over the cool and damp part of the evening. The night we put the filly down was no exception. The Evil Man had waited for the perfect time to act.

I rolled back the barn door and let the dogs go off their chains. I tapped the gas lamp that hung over a hook at the near end of shed row, got it on. I could hear the immensity of the horses rising from the hay in the stalls, the thud of hooves landing beneath their weight, and the sound of hay giving way and complaining while curious horses began to stick their heads over the webbing of their stalls to get a view of shed row. I walked toward the filly's stall dragging a sledge hammer with a wooden handle. The handle was as smooth as the handle of a baseball bat tooled by a lathe.

"No, not with that," Henry cried.

"It will be quick. I promise," I whispered. "Besides, you have the Derringer."

I don't know where I found the gumption to tell that lie. I had no idea what we were up against. I had no right to confidently promise anything. I had never put down a horse. I was too scared to even think of killing anything. I didn't even like to think about death.

The Horse

Back on the farm, I wasn't like the other boys. I didn't delight in chasing pigs to catch them for the slaughter. The pigs had instincts. They knew to squeal and run. I watched in horror as the men skillfully slit their unlucky throats and purple blood pulsed free of the pigs' quivering bodies. I closed my eyes shut hoping it could make that reality go away. The reality of farm life, the moment when chickens were separated from their heads on chopping blocks and the other forms of slaughter common to farm life, was a reality that never faded. I never had the stomach for any of it.

I didn't even have the stomach to club the field mice that built nests in the barn and spooked the horses. Nevertheless, I saw that cease and desist order as the filly's death warrant, so I dragged that sledge hammer off toward the filly's stall. Revenge is the strongest drug of all.

****

Henry followed with the burlap sack we used as a hood to calm unruly horses. I admit to being blinded by revenge to the point where I only saw parts of the scene, the horseman turned kingpin. I saw Henry throwing up a bottle of whiskey. He drained it.

On sleepless nights, the whole terrible scene comes back to me. It plays out in my mind over and over again, every thud of the sledgehammer and drop of blood plays out in agonizing slowness. I am afraid I shall be stuck with the poverty of the "spot" I was in, the horror of it, until the end of my days. That is the reason I prefer to tell the story quickly now.

****

I fiddled with a gas lamp hanging from a hook along shed row just outside the filly's stall, got it on. The glow lit the entire far end of the barn straight up to the rafters, and the flickering light mirrored in the filly's eyes as she stared back dumbly at us over the webbing of her stall. The spirit of a horse is found in the eyes, and the spirit commands the rest of the body into motion. In many ways, the spirit is separate from the body from the day a horse is foaled.

I hefted the sledgehammer. It is a tool with a nasty disposition. *Let this go quickly and without noise or much blood.*

I swung into the filly's stall. She backed away from the sledgehammer the same way pigs have the instinct to run and squeal long before the slaughter begins. She pinned back her ears and flashed the wild white of her eyes. She didn't rear, but her feet became nervous.

The wind had its way with the hay in the stall at the gaps between slats at the bottom of the stall. I could see the dark of night through those slats, and this caused me to remember the dogs. I worried the dogs might commence barking to sound the alarm if they were close enough to hear what was going on inside of that stall, but it was too late. The blood had already begun to pump rapidly through my body. The Evil Man had already taken over.

I told Henry to hand over the bag and motioned him to stand at the ready in front of the webbing outside the stall door. A weird thought came to me: We were the filly's only link to the humanity she had come to rely upon for her food, her shelter, and her glory as a champion over the Saratoga trotting course, and the filly would soon learn the terrible dark side of that same humanity.

Please let the sack hide the terrible reality of the act, I thought.

I stuffed the filly's muzzle in the bag and pulled it up over her ears. She tossed her head gently under the bag, but complied. Mine were the hands that had fed her, bathed her, brushed her, adored her. She seemed resigned to resist her instincts, the simple imperative to repel the threat of an attack. She had no reason to distrust me.

The filly snorted passionately against the burlap. Henry watched from outside the stall when I began to swing the handle. The head of the sledgehammer followed the arc. The weight of it had begun to negotiate its own volition. I could feel the weight of it cut cleanly through the air.

The first blow missed the filly's head, but landed flush against her neck. She whinnied and screamed. She reared and thrashed wildly. Her skull nearly hit the rafters. Her hooves beat against the air. I fell backward. The burlap sack fell away.

I saw the flash of fear in the wild white of her eyes. Her front legs thrashed so wildly I couldn't hold my stance. I had no target for the next blow. I swung anyway. I missed. She reared again teetering on her hind hooves. I hoped it wouldn't take too long, and there wouldn't be much blood.

She fought the attack with her screams and thrashing hooves. She threw up her front legs, reared, and twisted away. She whinnied and complained. I both fumbled and collected the sledgehammer in the same motion. I threw the head of it at her ankles and missed, like I might have slung that wooden shaft if it was a chain. The immensity of the beast touched down lightly on all four feet, and all four feet danced nervously on the hay searching for a way out of the attack. I threw again. The sledgehammer connected with the cavity at the top of her hips and beneath her tail. A stream of urine left her body and then a stream of blood.

I swung again and again. The head of the sledgehammer landed with a thud against her hip. She galloped into the wall in a desperate plea to escape. The tiny stall was little more than a jail cell. She tried to climb the wall on her front hooves to free herself of confinement. There was no escape. There was only the fury of the onslaught. The filly showed her teeth and whinnied. The filly consulted her instincts to rear yet again. The front legs climbed at the air, like the air was her salvation.

In the thrashing, there was also no target for Henry's Derringer. There was a moving target at best. I swung wildly and luckily struck a glancing blow against the filly's mouth that had dropped partially open in terror. There was the pop of fractured teeth and a red foam formed on her rubbery lips. Wounded, she stopped moving as wildly. She dropped her head to the hay as a sign of surrender. It was a ploy. The filly picked up her head again and tried to bolt. There was only one way out. It was over me and through the stall door toward the gas lamp. She lowered her head and charged.

I drove her back by jamming the sledgehammer under her jaw and into her throat latch, which threw her entire skull upward. The filly seemed confused. The hand that fed her was now the hand that tried to kill her. I swung again and again at the target her skull had become, and there was the thud of iron bouncing against bone again and again. The filly screamed. She suffered. It was not an easy kill.

"Stop!" Henry shrieked. I didn't stop. I couldn't stop. I didn't know how to stop. It was useless.

I didn't see or hear Henry. I also didn't hear the dogs. I only knew the Evil Man inside would hear nothing of the plea. The Evil Man had taken over. The Evil Man would carry on for as long as it took. The screams, the blood, the pop of fractured teeth only further excited the unmentionable parts of the Evil Man's soul.

Each time the sledgehammer landed, the filly whinnied and quivered, almost whimpered like a child.

"How much longer?" Henry cried.

I don't know, I thought. I might have said it aloud. I simply don't remember, but the rest of it is so clear that it haunts me.

I closed my eyes and hefted the weight of the sledgehammer over my head. The weight of it carried me to my toes and the head stood at the apex of the arc, motionless in the yellow light, and then I brought the sledgehammer down upon its target with all of the might I could summon as though the filly was an iron spike. I am not sure what I hit or if I hit. I know the filly screamed. One of her hooves clipped my right hand, and I am not sure how it happened from the filly's defeated, vulnerable posture. I stumbled away. There was blood.

I made an even tighter fist on that smooth handle and swung again. This time I am sure I clipped her right shin with the flat face of that angry tool. This put the filly down.

The slender bones of her stricken right leg folded over in two, like a broken pendulum of a case clock. She tried to use it to scratch at the floor as she laid flopped hopelessly over on her side and tried to rise. She hadn't figured out the mystery of it. The leg had become a useless stump. The rounded cheek of her face was now stationary and exposed on the floor. Her belly heaved, begged for air. She groaned with eyes wide open.

"Now!" I implored Henry to act.

Henry swung into the stall. The Derringer was in his hand. He pressed the barrel against the flesh over the filly's eye. He triggered the weapon. There was an explosion. The ball sent a spray of blood into the air and made a mess of the filly's eye. She was gone.

Her body rolled against the bottom plank of the stall facing the outside world. That was simply fortuitous. The night air would ward off any telltale odors and sweep olfactory evidence out of the barn.

I realized the spray of blood from the gunshot had splattered against my face and dripped from my eyebrows, nose, and lips. I used the burlap to wipe my face free of the blood. I handed the burlap to Henry. He did the same.

Then, I heard the barking and yelping of the dogs.

The filly's chestnut coat had already begun to turn a blackish-purple with the blood. Henry froze and stared at our defeated champion. I unhooked the stall door latch.

"Hurry, you have to help me if you don't want to go to prison. You have to help me dig the hole and hide the evidence," I said, looking down shed row toward the tack room at the far end of the barn. "Hurry. We got to dig a hole. We got to bury her."

I staggered out of the stall. The deed was done. I let the dogs into the barn to quiet them. They wagged their tails with their tongues lolling. The dogs didn't seem to appreciate the gravity of the hour.

We grabbed two flat shovels and began digging and clearing away space in the empty stall. The flat shovels were excellent tools to muck out stalls and toss around soiled hay, but they weren't a grave digger's tool. They made the work laborious and slow. We had

The Horse

no choice. We had to use them. We dug desperately. The work was going quite slow.

I put a lantern on a hook in the stall which cast eerie shadows everywhere.

We picked, dug, slung, and sweated in that stall. We hustled to complete the grave before the morning light. Sunrise would bring the new owners and possibly the authorities to execute the order. We would lie. We would tell them the filly had been turned out, escaped. They were free to send a search party after her. But if there was any trace of the crime, they would take custody of our bodies on the "spot."

We moved a small mound of earth to the left side of the grave. The straw was piled high on the right. When the hole was two feet deep, just enough depth to make a dead horse disappear, we stopped, moped our brows, and looked for whiskey. Of course, Henry knew exactly where to find it.

"We have time before sunrise," I said.

"That horse suffered."

"Mr. Tripps made her suffer."

"Mr. Tripps did not swing that sledgehammer."

"And Mr. Tripps didn't pull the trigger of that Derringer."

"What if I tell?'

"What?"

"Oh, nothing. Bad timing for a joke."

"If you tell, we will both go to prison. You for knocking up a little girl. Me for killing a horse."

The lines of betrayal had been drawn. The Evil Man cared only that Henry knew his role as an accessory. On second thought, he could no longer be considered an accessory. He pulled the trigger. That made him the principal. The Evil Man was happy. He didn't care about the glossary of terms in a law book. The Evil Man cared only that he had scored revenge against Mr. Tripps, and the precious filly would get rolled into a shallow grave.

We kept digging. The hole was more than three feet deep. There was plenty of depth to bury the carcass and level the top soil. The carcass twitched. I froze and watched. Gangrene had set in. I hadn't been aware that gangrene caused twitching. The filly's legs were frozen stiff. There was no twitching there. Tubular pink entrails had already begun to ooze out of the filly's rectum. The stench was oppressive. I began to question what I saw. Did the filly actually *twitch*? The corpse exhaled. I told myself it was the final breath. It smelled of alfalfa, the filly's last meal. Henry let out a terrible laugh.

"She won't come back to life to haunt us, will she?" Henry laughed.

"Nonsense."

I was wrong. I knew I was wrong. This was a ghost story. Of course, there would be a ghost. The filly was dead, so who, or what, do you think would be the most likely candidate to play the role of the ghost? Henry wasn't the brightest bloke in the world. It didn't take very much talent to knock up a local girl, but I would have figured he'd have gotten the identity of the ghost right on the very first try.

We looked in on the filly. She was still pressed against the back of her stall. Busy flies crowded what remained of the filly's wounded eye. We spread blankets on the floor. We grabbed the filly's ankles in each hand and rolled the body over onto the blankets. We each took up a corner of the blanket and dragged the weight of the dead filly. A dog barked, and Henry jumped.

He dropped the blanket and laughed. He composed himself and kept working. We dragged the filly completely out of the stall and across shed row. I stooped over the filly to get a tighter hold on the corner of the blanket. I felt something brush the cuff of my pants.

It was a baby raccoon at my feet. The raccoon's face was covered in blood. It had stringy pink mucous stuck in its delicate claws. The raccoon clung to my pant leg like a toddler clings to a parent for affection. I screamed and kicked the claws free. The raccoon fled.

We dragged the filly to the hole and yanked and heaved against the weight of the blanket. The corpse began to roll. Its long neck flopped the weight of the head over and over again. The muzzle was pointed upward to the rafters, so the open eyeball seemed to stare at us.

We shoveled hard and fast to lustily throw dirt at the filly in the hole to try to make her go away, until all but the head was covered. I began to think how things would have turned out differently if Mr. Tripps had been reasonable, correct, fair, just. The dirt covered the filly up to her shoulders. The neck and head remained above ground, like an obscene vegetable.

The cloud of flies around the filly's eyes were relentless and aggressive, like the pests were somehow aware it was their last clear chance to feed. The filly's neck was twisted by the weight of the head. I wondered how many last breaths this filly had. She does have rather huge lungs.

"You critter," Henry screamed.

Henry's shovel whistled past my face. It bounced off a raccoon running freely along the back wall of the stall. The raccoon yelped and fled into the darkness.

"These coons are everywhere in here," Henry said, grinning inappropriately. The grin dissolved into a level of obscene laughter, not the ordinary laughter one expects to hear in a barn or anywhere in society, but the laughter one expects to hear behind locked doors in a sanitarium.

"You're just spooked. They come when they smell a slaughter. The same thing happens when you slaughter pigs on the farm."

He didn't bother to retrieve the shovel. He staggered into the door frame of the stall and looked at what was left of the filly above ground. He stared at the filly and then up at me. "Are you sure Alexander?"

Of course, I am not sure. I am lying about the whole thing to shut you up, I thought. "Of course, I am sure. You nailed that critter. I am sure of that. I heard the thud. It is long gone thanks to you."

Henry grinned. Thankfully, the laughter was long gone, too.

The filly's rubbery lips began to twitch. I stopped everything and stared at her mouth. I scarcely believed my eyes. I waited to see if she twitched again. I began to wonder how gangrene could make such an immense jaw twitch. I swore I saw the entire jaw move as if to chew. My mind remained safely in denial. But the jaw was indeed moving. It was undeniable. It worked open so the dentures showed, and the shoulder and arm of an adult raccoon reached out for the open air.

The raccoon's head was covered with blood. Its fur was matted and wet. The rest of its body followed, like the filly's mouth was birthing the wretched feline.

The raccoon stood upright on the grave, but it didn't flee. It chewed and stared, unafraid. I threw the shovel at it and missed. The raccoon ran, but it didn't escape cleanly. It crashed into my leg on its way out the stall door. I danced away and shook my leg, even after the raccoon had already escaped to shed row.

"Those coons got to the stench of the filly while we were digging. Must have smelled her and got in through the slats in the stall," I reasoned. The raccoons didn't bother me. What bothered me is the reason the raccoons chose to contact me and not Henry. Was it deliberate?

"God are you sure?"

"Whatever else is left is getting buried alive."

The raccoon was gone, but the filly remained. The filly's eyes stared away. I decided it was necessary to cover the filly's head with the burlap sack. It was the sort of irrational decision that only makes perfect sense in the middle of chaos. I guess I figured covering the head would make it go away. When I stooped to affix the hood, the filly exhaled in my face. The stench was wretched. This wasn't the sweet smell of alfalfa and open fields. It was the stench of bloated slugs dead and floating on the murky water of ancestral ponds. I fought to retain my dignity, but lost. I belched and disgorged. I used the palms of my hands against my knees to steady the weight of my upper body, convulsed, and let loose a spray of yellow and orange vomit. I recognized my dinner and the little whiskey I had drunk from Henry's glass bottle on the floor and over the tops of my boots.

I wiped off my lips with the sleeve of my gown, retrieved the shovel, and shoveled fast and hard, violently kicking the filly's head and threw as much dirt at the filly's eyes as I could. Bizarrely, I chose to blame the filly for the vomit. What was left of the filly vanished beneath a blanket of loose soil. I tamped the dirt over the grave with the flat blade of the shovel. We smoothed out the top soil with our boots like a baseball batter smooths out the dirt in the batter's box, and piled fresh hay over the grave. There would be no credible evidence. I put my face to the lamp and got it out.

I apologized to the filly for the first time. The filly replied: *History cannot be unlived, but it can be paid for. I'll accept that vomit on your shoes as your down payment.*

We went to the tack room. I sat on the upholstered wing chair with the springs beneath the seat. Henry opened the cabinet where the bottles of poultice, liniment, and bandages were stored looking for hidden whiskey.

There was the rustling of the brass on a pile of loose tack in the corner of the room. Henry busied himself in the cabinet, pulled down a whiskey bottle. The seal was still intact. He opened it with his molars.

A grown raccoon brushed against the cuff of my pant leg from its hiding place in the darkness. Its grey furry tail lashed at my leg like a whip and wrapped around my ankles as it fled. Its enormous head popped up between my legs from under the seat of the wing chair. I sprung to my feet. I kicked the critter away with composure and dignity, or so I thought.

The raccoon ran to the tack room door in a bid to escape. Oddly, it got to the door and instead of fleeing to join the others, he dared to stop, stand, and turn to face me. This shook my composure. I tried to yell, but the most embarrassing, effeminate shriek issued from a small place in my emotions I didn't even know existed. I swear the raccoon glared at me for an instant like it was trying to make up its mind about what to do next, thought better of it, and fled.

"What the... We got an infestation of them things somewhere in the barn," Henry said, swigging the whiskey bottle.

"The sense of death must have brought them circling like vultures." *Or was it the sense of resurrection?*

Relieved, I flopped on the seat of the upholstered chair. When the springs under the seat complained, a great crowd of the raccoon's relatives rushed from the tack pile toward the door. One of them had something pinkish red smeared across its face. I threw the chair at the entire crowd, but the felines nimbly escaped, unscathed. The chair tumbled uselessly over and over again, stopping with the chair legs upright and the seat whirling. My mind roared with disgust. I chased after them outside the room and into the dirt of shed row. The dogs barked as the felines swirled out of the far end of the barn.

As I stooped to pick up the chair, I wondered how much of it I had imagined, especially the *twitches*. I learned something that night that most people never dare to imagine: the same humanity that nurtures and protects the inherent dignity, majesty really, of a being is equally capable of cavorting with the Evil Man, giving in to his demands, conspiring with him, and doing his work, and when it is finished, it has remarkably little difficulty haunting him.

Then, Henry started in with me. "That was something we did that will send us straight to Hell. I am sure of it. The coons are a sign of it."

"A sign of what?"

"Killing that filly. She was innocent. She did nothing to us."

"It is a thing decided. It is done. Leave it alone. Done is done."

"The cemetery is full of people who think done is done. There is a special place in Hell for this kind of logic."

"We are already in Hell, Henry. We can worry about Hell later on when we get to the afterlife. In this life, we better worry about prison and nothing else."

"Do you think we'll end up in prison?"

"Jail yes, prison no," I joked.

"What?"

"No. I'm only joking. I've got that one covered."

"You've got that one covered! You've got that one covered! Henry laughed. "From where I am standing, it don't look like you've got nothing covered! We've got one dead filly covered, alright, buried. The only thing you've got covered is the filly's dead body covered in dirt. "

The Evil Man wanted to raise the flat side of the shovel blade and bring it down against Henry's skull. The timing for that was wrong. Besides, the facts had an elegant way of speaking for themselves. The idea of revenge was not new. However, it was my fault that

The Horse

we killed the filly as a form of revenge against Mr. Tripps. *Except the coons,* I thought. *I am responsible for the filly and everything else, everything else, that is, but not the coons. I have no idea how they got into the picture.* A voice laughed inside my head. *There are probably more coons that were buried inside the filly having a merry old time right now chewing away on the tasty parts.*

"Are we ever going to move the filly's body?" Henry asked.

"Not now. There will be an investigation."

****

Two days later, there was an investigation. The fancy new owners didn't show up to enforce the order. It was the sheriff. He dismounted and moseyed up to the barn door. He peeked inside.

"I am here to pick up the horse," he said, chewing away on a chaw of tobacco.

"What horse?" I asked, walking out of the shadows of the barn and jamming my hands into my pockets. The sheriff's deputy came up on a galloping horse to join the investigation. There was a cloud of dust. He pulled up his mount short of the barn door, leaned into the saddle horn, and stayed up in the saddle.

"Come on, Alex, the filly," the sheriff insisted.

"Gone," I said.

"What did you do with her?"

"Nothing."

"Nothing? So how is she gone?"

"She unlatched her stall door with her teeth, walked down shed row on her own in the middle of the night while we were asleep in the tack room I might add," I said, referring to Henry who came blinking into the sunlight from the barn, "freed every horse in here by pulling open their stall latches one by one, and walked straight out that door at the end of the bar. When I woke up in the morning, the filly was gone. Most of the horses wandered around outside the barn for a while and came back in, but the filly didn't come back. She's gone."

"That's an elaborate story."

"I've heard of that happening before in other barns," offered the deputy, still on his mount.

"They'll never believe that story," said the sheriff.

"Don't matter what they believe. Matters what happened," I said.

"You Henry?" The sheriff looked over Henry from head to toe, like he was searching Henry for answers, like the answers were written in script and concealed somewhere on his clothing. "Where'd you spend the night?"

The Horse

"Town." Henry lied. That one word signaled there was no longer any chance Henry would, or could, betray me.

"By the way, you wouldn't happen to know nothing about that Greeley girl, would you?" The sheriff stopped searching and made eye contact with Henry, chewing on the tobacco at a speed to keep up with the thoughts that were going through his mind.

"What do you mean?" Henry asked.

"Oh, suppose not. Never mind. That's a different case. This ain't over. I can only go to the judge and inform him I couldn't execute the order. The judge ain't gonna be happy. I can tell you that. I'm sure I'll be back." The sheriff walked over to his mount, grabbed the saddle horn, stuck his boot in the irons, and threw himself up into the saddle.

"Come back when you got some facts to go on, hear?"

The sheriff didn't ask his mount to move, not yet. Instead, he looked past me, like he was trying to make his mind up on what, if anything, to say next.

"Oh, by the way, the law says that filly is only property," I said. My pride forced me to keep talking. "It ain't no human life, so you can't kidnap it, which ain't no crime."

"You may not be able to kidnap a horse, but you can steal one. That's a crime. That's grand larceny. Day," the sheriff said, turning away his mount. The deputy turned away his mount, too.

****

The sheriff returned the next day. He tied off his mount, walked over to the edge of the barn door, and waited. On the ground, he was a stocky man with short, fat fingers. The silver five-pointed star pinned on his snowy white dress shirt made him relevant. He used his thumbs to snap his braces. This gave his round belly more space to operate.

"Help you?" I walked into the sunlight, squinting.

"The judge sent me back to have a look around the barn."

"You mean search the place for the filly?"

"Yup. Law says you got a right to say no."

"I know what the law says. Told you the filly ain't here."

"The judge said I was dumb not to conduct a search last time I was here. I don't want the judge to get into the habit of calling me dumb. It ain't good for job security, if you know what I mean. I am sorry to trouble you a second time…"

The Horse

"I know you're just doing your job, sheriff. I got a job to do, too. Think you'd recognize the filly even if you laid eyes on her?"

"Probably not."

"Step inside and search away, sheriff."

We stepped aside, and we walked into the shadows inside the barn together. Henry happened to be leading a horse toward us on shed row at the same time, walking. The sheriff started to wander on the wrong side of the horse as it dragged its heavy hooves along through the dirt.

"Hold on there, sheriff," I said, calmly grabbing his arm, "never on the right side of the horse. Always stay to the left side."

"Oh, sorry."

"That's to keep you from getting kicked. If the horse acts up, if the horse kicks, Henry can just turn the horse toward us on this side, and the feet are going off in the opposite direction away from us. On the other side, that doesn't work. If she kicks you with those hooves, they'll hit you with the same force as that big gun you got there, sheriff."

The other horses along shed row watched the spectacle over the webbing at their stall doors. Some horses chewed hay, and others didn't, but they all stared.

The horses didn't act up. They didn't seem particularly interested in the way the sheriff's chaw or his crotch smelled. One of the dogs came up and sniffed up and down the sheriff's leg.

The sheriff moseyed down shed row looking at the horse in each stall. "What'd she look like anyway?"

"A chestnut with a white blaze," I said, catching the confused look on the sheriff's face. "Er, a light brown horse with a white spot on her face."

"None of these look like that."

That's because she's dead and buried beneath the floor, genuis, I thought. "Told yuh she ain't here. She's none of these."

The sheriff looked at the one empty stall in the barn. "What's in here? What's this one for?"

That's a graveyard. We use this space to bury dead fillies, I thought. "That's an empty stall. We get a boarder. We board here. In the meantime, we got mares in foal. If we can foal outside in the open air, of course, that's the best place to foal, but if we get rain, and it seems like it rains every day in Saratoga, we foal 'em in here."

Would he go outside the barn and look around out back? Would he search the dirt on the floor to look for drag marks, mounds, depressions, hoof prints, boot prints, blood, anything? Would he conduct a real search? Would he look for signs something had changed or had been moved or was amiss if he was a real sheriff and not just some hick from Ballston Spa or wherever he was from?

"Oh," he said.

Oh, what? You don't even know what I am talking about. If you asked questions instead walking around like an authority, or even if you kicked at the dirt, the filly planted in the open stall there might actually twitch or a coon or two might make a surprise visit. That might make for one excellent case, I thought.

There was a big gun on his hip. I didn't like being around big guns, the threat of them, the unspoken message. I also didn't like being around silver five-pointed stars and placed in the position of defending myself against someone trained to believe he held all of the cards. I wanted to deflect the feeling that washed over me.

"I am surprised you're here without a search warrant. I am not saying I need one," I shrugged. "I am just saying."

The sheriff dumbly shrugged back. "I know. The law-abiding folks rarely ask for paperwork. You being that sort probably never heard of Judge John C. Hulbert. But Judge Hulbert is what you'd call a royal pain in the you know what. I don't need him berating me over and over again about this horse, whether I did this right or that right. Everybody knows the law ain't good for nobody except rich folks. The fools are out there right now fighting a civil war for rich folks who worry about racehorses a whole lot more than warhorses or war casualties."

The words spoken were not put together in an intelligent way, but the sheriff was far from dumb. The homey types lull you into walking into the trap of underestimation, a very short and tricky walk for a man who had only recently buried a filly.

"Maybe we can invite Judge Hulbert to the barn to have a look around himself. We'll let him walk on the wrong side of all of the horses he sees," I laughed and winked.

The sheriff let loose a laugh that threatened to bother the horses: Hawh, hawh, hawh! But his eyes weren't laughing. They were peeking, prying, and searching. With that, he walked back into the sunlight at the front end of the barn.

"I'll probably be back," he said.

Henry stopped and watched the sheriff turn his mount away. He looked at the dirt of shed row while the sheriff rode off.

"Do you think he'll be back?" I asked Henry. I wanted to prompt him and to have a look into his mind.

"Probably," he said, still looking at the ground.

"Probably is right. Do you think you'll be here when he does?"

"Probably," Henry said colorlessly.

I smiled. The Evil Man had learned the truth. Henry's colorless reply meant he planned to abandon the "spot," which was fine. The sooner he left, the less chance he had of giving the authorities a conflicting account of what happened to the filly.

****

The Greeley girl lived on her father's dairy farm in Ballston Spa. Henry halted the coach and two horses he stole from the livery in Saratoga. He hopped down just outside of the property line and approached the house on foot. The moon lit everything, except the shadows beneath trees and behind the house and barn.

Henry got to within thirty yards of the house, give or take, and stopped. He stood along the trunk of a tree, waiting. There was silence, except for the *reeee* of crickets.

This wasn't a turkey shoot, but Henry knew how to yelp and cluck to call turkeys out of the bush. He used this talent to send a signal. He let loose a turkey call up to the Greely girl's bedroom window. Then, he made himself small against the trunk of a tree and waited.

The linen curtains before one of the upstairs windows swung away. After the reeee of crickets closed in from several directions, he heard the breathless excitement of the Greeley girl escaping the house into the moonlight. Her white nightgown glowed and billowed in the moonlight as she raced toward the tree that hid Henry. The sound of her bare feet beating the earth grew closer and closer, until she was swept into Henry's arms. They hungrily kissed, careful to leave enough space between them for her pregnancy.

"Why are you here?"

"I am here because it is time. We have to run now while we still can. We can't hide any longer."

"Why?"

"Why! You're pregnant. We have to run to save the child."

"Save the child from what?"

"Them. All of them. This is no place to raise a child, not this child, don't you agree? This place has a disease for a child like our child. They are fighting a war right now over that disease. What do you think they'll do to us? If we get gone, we can have this child together in peace."

"In peace?"

"In peace."

"Together?"

"Together."

"Run, but where?"

"We got to get away from here, maybe Canada. We can find safe haven in Skaneateles…"

"Where?"

"Skaneateles, a place in the Finger Lakes. I've heard they have rail links there. You can have the baby there, and we can make it North."

They climbed onto the box. Henry shook the reins at the horses. They disappeared into the darkest parts of the woods around Ballston Spa.

****

I was the one who had convinced Henry to run. I had a way with his mind. I, or should I say the Evil Man, knew how to exploit his weaknesses. It was easy to convince him to follow the weakness of his flesh, gather up the Greeley girl, and spirit her out of the county. I told him he didn't stand a chance anywhere near Saratoga, not during a civil war, not ever. I implored him to do the responsible thing, the manly thing. If he fled, he could find lodging for both of them and the charity of a midwife. This would buy them time to decide if the child looked white enough for the Catholic Church to perform a proper adoption, an adoption with an adoring couple who could offer a newborn a suitable future. If not, they could make it North, even across the border into Canada if necessary, and make a go at raising the child alone.

"But I am leaving you to handle what we did to the filly alone," Henry said.

"You didn't kill the filly. I did."

"We killed the filly together."

"I put you up to it. That makes me the provocateur. Get gone, boy. Take your woman and get gone. I won't implicate you in any of this if the noose tightens. Don't worry, boy."

I lied. I wasn't convinced Henry would hold up under interrogation, if an interrogation ever made its way to our "spot." I saw Henry as the type who would crack. He would give in. He would confess. He might even cry while doing so.

There was something pathetic and meek in his manic laughter. It might have been triggered by the mere sight of felines. If he laid eyes on a big gun and tricky questioning, at worst he would give a full written confession, and at best he would give away factual detail that would allow the tricky lawyers behind the sheriff enough information to fill in the blanks. The Evil Man wanted Henry gone at all costs, not for the protection of the pregnant little slut he had impregnated, assuming, of course, that he, and not some clumsy, pimple-faced

The Horse

school chum of our little princess, turned out to be the child's biological father, but for the protection of the Evil Man.

Henry agreed reluctantly. "That judge will put us both in jail or worse, and my child will be born without his pa. I don't want to go to no jail." His eyes watered.

"Nobody's going to jail." *But that little slut's old man and a wagon-full of his chums might make jail seem like Paradise. They might hang your hide from a tree, take a knife to your genitals, and watch the flames lick at your flesh until it drips and cracks. Those boys have smelled flesh burn before. They are not likely to take kindly to anyone knocking up their little girl, certainly not a colored groom*, I thought. "Drive that wagon to the Quakers in the Finger Lakes. The Quakers will take you in."

And so I fell asleep in the tack room alone that night. Henry was off to Ballston Spa to kidnap the Greeley girl, the owls hunted, the raccoons prowled, the dogs barked, and the filly was planted in complete darkness in a shallow grave under a haymow with the back of her head blown wide open and her brain exposed to maggots and whatever else thrives upon the rotten flesh of the fallen. The next day the sun came up, the horses were fed, and Henry sat on a wagon with the

Greeley girl's hair looking a mess, like a raccoon had become entangled in it.

****

If good works are as filthy rags in the sight of the Lord – the Old Testament is full of catchy aphorisms that lead to vindication, and Saint Augustine certainly made sport of arguing the case for vindication – then I simply cannot imagine the horrors that await those of us who are guilty of bad works. I know I face punishment, and I figure it must be bad, but I can't say for sure. I wonder if there is mitigation or even outright mercy anywhere. I can say for sure that the Evil Man lured me into doing it. I can say for sure that the summer we put down the filly was extraordinary with no hint of fall or the cruelty of winter in the air. There was heat and sun and endless blue skies that would leave orange and yellow stains on the hills with the coming of fall.

I had worried that Judge Hulbert would send the sheriff knocking again, but he didn't. If Henry made it to the Quakers in the Finger Lakes with the Greeley girl, I imagined he probably had become a proud father by now. If you know your history, you know most of the South was vexed over what Mr. Lincoln characterized as an insurrection, which was news to the Confederate soldiers who were fighting it. By

The Horse

1863, the farmers along the Eastern Seaboard resisted the federal government in every way imaginable, but it had already become clear that cutting rail links could only delay the steady advance of Union troops. Like the filly, the Confederacy was destined to return to the very same dust known to *Isaiah*, but unlike the filly, the Confederacy would eventually give up the fight. The filly refused to surrender or forgive, and I'll get to telling you more about that soon.

Miss Heath, Mr. Tripps's lady friend, visited the barn twice that summer. I figured she was a spy for Mr. Tripps, until she advised of their separation. He left for Philadelphia. She remained behind in Saratoga, alone, and free to explore society.

She visited the barn in the early morning. The dogs sniffed at the curiosity of her unmentionable parts between her legs, until I sheepishly shooed them away. The riding britches and high boots made her desire to get on a horse for a gallop sort of obvious. The hair tied up in a bun and the man's blouse she wore made the essence of her womanhood less obvious, until I gave her a leg up and she opened her mount up into a gentle gallop. This made her ample bodice leap about.

The second time she came to the barn she came right out with it: What happened to the filly? Did you sell it? Why hasn't it turned up at a stable somewhere, a precious commodity like her? I know you hate Mr. Tripps. He has a way of inspiring hatred.

"Miss Heath, if you're asking me if I sold the filly, the answer is no."

"I didn't figure you'd admit to anything, not to me. I split with him a long time ago, couldn't stand the arrogance. Just wondering. She was precious."

I'd take the flat blade of one of them shovels to the side of your skull and drop you into the same hole the filly's in, since you're so concerned. But that would bring this whole affair to a much different level. Besides, I rather enjoy watching you bouncing around on top of a racehorse. It gives me a little something to fantasize over after my chores are done, and I am lying awake late at night, I thought. "I didn't do nothing to that filly," I lied.

"I don't care nothing about Charlie's property really anyway, certainly not after we split."

"Why exactly did you split, if you don't mind me asking?"

"He caught me dead in the act with one of my lady lovers, bloomers and all. He wouldn't dream of scandalizing his name by reporting the infidelity to anyone. I begged him to see things my way and keep the relationship together. I asked him to just hit me to forgive the transgression. So, obliged. He struck me

The Horse

with the butt of his Derringer's pearl handle, but a man like Charlie never ever forgives. Our romance was over except the sobbing, my sobbing. A man like Charlie is afraid to possess an open mind. Are you?" I didn't answer Miss Heath. I didn't know how. I didn't want to know how.

When we got back to the tack room after her gallop around the trotting course, the flies were busy at the air. I offered Miss Heath a swig off one of Henry's whiskey bottles. I sat on the upholstered wing chair. She fiddled with the tack, looking at the different bridles and hoods. I don't remember exactly how it got started, but it got started. Miss Heath was riding double with me on the upholstered wing chair. The springs beneath the seat complained louder and louder. A couple of dogs looked sideways at the spectacle of it.

When it was over, Miss Heath gathered up her possessions and said nothing. I still wonder whether cutting Miss Heath loose on society opened up her curiosities and whether I was a simple curiosity, or was it strictly a case of revenge against Mr. Tripps? Either way, revenge takes many different forms, doesn't it?

****

Henry hadn't taken the Greeley girl directly to the Quakers. He decided instead to make a stop along the way. Turns out, an evil man had made it inside of him, too.

He smashed the plate glass front of the First National Bank of Syracuse. The legal papers filed later would accurately reflect that the heist began only minutes after the bank was closed for business at 3 o'clock. Henry didn't know anything about how to pull off a job like that. He didn't have to. He was wearing a big gun at the time. The girl waited up on the box. The whole job took less than two minutes.

When Henry returned to the coach, he had a bag full of Confederate currency, scrip, and left behind a bank full of witnesses and a dead teller. The big gun had been triggered. The barrel was still hot. The bank teller was on the floor with a ball lodged somewhere in a region of his brain just north of the right eyebrow.

Henry screamed at the horses and shook the reins. They got away from the bank in a cloud of dust. They traveled nonstop over hill and dale, unhooking the coach, and riding away to the outskirts of town.

****

I walked around the barn in a daze. I knew when Henry left Saratoga he would learn just how cruel the world was to a colored groom, especially one brazen enough to cavort with a pregnant white girl. I lost track

The Horse

of my chores. For the first time since Judge Hulbert sent the sheriff out to the barn to ask polite questions that instantly became churlish and clumsily loaded while searching everything, jail or worse, a lynch mob, seemed like a real possibility, so real I could almost hear the iron gates swing closed and lock with cold finality and the laughter of a lynch mob urging me into the deepest forest with a noose already swinging around my neck like a heavy necklace.

Henry was a lock to fail whether he was lynched or not. That seemed inevitable. Two horses could only pull a load so far without provisions. A pregnant girl was quite unlikely to survive very long on horseback. If he tried to use the Derringer to rob a farmer along the way, he'd more than likely get hunted down and apprehended. I suspected if Henry was cornered and held by the authorities, he would eventually figure out that he could turn on me and use Mr. Tripps as an extravagant bargaining tool. Mr. Tripps certainly could use his influence to settle Henry's trouble in exchange for information that got to the bottom of how the filly disappeared.

My only hope was that, once arrested, Henry would remain silent and realize it was the weakness of his flesh alone that led him to cavort with the Greeley girl, and his flesh had nothing at all to do with the bad blood that led to the demise of the filly. Hoping for a colored groom in the middle of the Civil War who had willingly and notoriously placed himself in this predicament suddenly developing sound judgment is rather like betting on long shots at the racetrack, but wasn't I in a terrible "spot" that was not likely to ever change?

As I carried a bucket of fresh water down shed row, unaware of the water slopping over the rim, a wild thought crossed my mind: pack a bag and make a run for Canada. The idea gained a momentum all its own, but it crashed squarely into the Evil Man who by now was quite a stern master. The Evil Man wanted me to stay in Saratoga, gut it out, maybe even claim more horse flesh along the way. I still had most of the money I made gambling on the filly to beat Captain Moore – 175 bucks to be exact – but the Evil Man was having none of it. Like so many others, the Evil Man was madly in love with Saratoga. The Evil Man tempted me by mentioning that Miss Heath, who he was now referring to as simply Fran, might decide to make another trip to the barn and hop on the old upholstered wing chair for another bareback ride. *Howdy do!* I thought.

The Evil Man argued the sheriff couldn't solve the case of the missing filly, even if the judge wrote out the questions to ask on a slip of paper and included a map drawn to scale to mark the exact places in and around the barn to search with large "X's." *The fool would probably only end up losing the script and map on the way over to the barn, standing around to seem important, scratching the back of his neck, eyeballing the horses while trying to remember what was written on the paper, and drawing blanks before giving up*, I thought. However, the idea didn't give up easily. It sidestepped the Evil Man and hung on. It mentioned I could skip across the border at quite a number of different places without any problem. I could take a pack horse, too. The railroad was another option. I convinced myself that this wasn't the important thing. I had destroyed the filly out of revenge, and I wasn't going to let change govern my actions because Henry had gotten it into his head to take off with his romantic interest. If I got caught crossing the border, it would be tantamount to an admission of guilt. And I could expect to find my way into a set of chains from there.

****

That was on a Monday. There was still no word on Tuesday or Wednesday of that week that Henry had been picked up on his way to the Quakers in Skaneateles with a kidnapped minor in tow who was seen wearing a white gown that billowed forth about the waist line in a most indisputably curious way. The Greeley girl would only need to mention her age to make out an indefensible case, but there was no word from the girl's father over in Ballston Spa or anyone else that the marshals in Skaneateles had thrown Henry into the pokey where he was telling wild tales about winning match races at Saratoga or beating off a retinue of raccoons long enough to bury a filly with a rather large entry wound over its right eyeball. All was quiet in the barn.

I mucked out the stalls, I swung into each stall to toss generous beds of fresh hay, I put down feed, I hung buckets of water on hooks outside of the stalls, I fed the dogs, I untangled tack – and I did it all in a fog. I began to slip into the belief that all of this was a long and terrible dream, and I would awake with the filly still happily in her stall and Mr. Tripps showering me with praise and cash for getting him to the winner's circle at Saratoga.

Then, on Thursday, the sheriff came by the barn and came right out with the key question: "Where's Henry, and where is the Greeley girl?"

He had either gotten smart overnight (unlikely), or the Greeley girl's father had made a trip to Saratoga to see the judge (likely).

The Horse

"Damned if I know."

"Seems like you'd know."

"Thank you for the compliment, but there's a lot I don't know."

"Obviously there's a lot none of us knows," he said, lowering his eyes and scratching the back of his neck, like the back of his neck could help him sort things out.

For the first time, the sheriff looked straight past me and down shed row at the horses. "Does your offer to let me look around still stand?" he asked, still looking at the horses like they were the members of a choir. "Of course, if you decline…"

"Guilty men decline. Law abiding folks…"

"Cooperate. Now, let's see if we can't straighten this mess out."

He stepped into the tack room. He looked at the tack hanging from a hook on the wall. He picked up bridles and tried to figure them out, like they were calculus problems. I tried to follow the ritual quietly: the eyes sweeping every inch of the tack room, the preoccupation with the back of his neck, the resting of the meaty palm of his hand on the butt of his big gun. I couldn't help myself. "Do you want to look around outside, too?"

"I'll get to that in a minute."

He surveyed shed row, looking into the face of every horse in the barn. The horses dumbly obliged by staring back at him, heads upright and steady over the webbing, eyes steady as well, ears twitching. The sheriff walked to the door at the rear of the barn, stopped short of venturing outside, deciding instead to survey the surroundings without setting foot outside. The dogs felt privileged to come up to him with tongues lolling and tails wagging and follow the scent of his crotch as he returned to the shadows of the barn enclosure and walked directly into the empty stall and stood over the gravesite, like a fierce spiritual magnet had drawn him there. He scratched the back of his neck again. "This is where you board, right?"

"Board and foal," I spit out the words, gasping. The sheriff was literally on the exact "spot" where the filly's head was last seen as a grotesque vegetable. I might only have imagined it, but the mound of hay under the sheriff's feet seemed to move, like the odd vegetable was growing in the mound and was about to break the top soil like a mound of potatoes gives way to lush green vines.

"Right. Board and foal." He kicked at the hay over the gravesite. "Seems like you ain't used it in a

The Horse

while." The hay mound gave way ever so slightly. I was sure of it.

Oh, we've used it plenty, sheriff, I thought. *God, if the filly smells or a coon with part of its lunch hanging from its whiskers pops up, there won't be much to figure out from there, will there?* "No, nope, we ain't got no foaling to do, and we ain't had no boarders all summer."

"Hmm..." He looked straight past me and down shed row at the horses again.

The sheriff scratched the back of his neck, and left without saying another word. If he had said something else, anything else, it would have given me something to work with, a group of words I could interpret, rearrange, speculate about hidden meanings, and rationalize in a way that all but made the sheriff's interest disappear, like a bag of marbles I could stare at long enough to convince myself that marbles are not round. But "hmm" is entirely different. It invites rank speculation. It plays tricks with the imagination, and my imagination had already become good friends with the Evil Man.

****

On Friday the sheriff came back, riding a nag that lazily dragged its hooves through the dust. The silver star worn on his vest caught the sunlight in a way that blinded my imagination. And he wasn't alone. Following alongside was a fancy man atop a fancy horse brushed to perfection with polished hooves. The fancy man wore a black waist coat, and the wind was having its way with his hair. My heart jumped around at the sight, then gurgled when I was sure who rode the fancy horse: Gerrit Smith, Esq., the local prosecutor.

I tried to wait calmly at the barn door while the arrival ceremony was underway: the sheriff would drag his right leg across the saddle and drop to the ground while still holding the reins; touch the butt of his big gun with the palm of his hand. I would be lucky if the prosecutor stayed up on his mount and only said *hmmm*, I thought. I lost my composure. "Is everything alright, Sheriff?"

"Not exactly," the sheriff said. Both the sheriff and the counselor swung their legs over their saddles and slid belly first to the ground. They looked at their boots as they walked. When they got closer to me, I could hear their breathing. They made eye contact briefly and looked past me at the barn. "I am getting a lot of paperwork about what's going on out here. I don't need no extra paperwork," the sheriff said, still looking at the barn.

The Horse

"Well, how can I help you, sheriff?" I had my hands in my pockets.

"You can help us by telling the truth," the counselor interrupted.

"I have."

"Look," the counselor took over, "we are in the middle of a civil war and got more important stuff to worry about than Tripps's horse."

"And now a missing Greeley girl," the sheriff added.

"I don't know what I can say to add to what I already said on it. I'd love to help you," I mumbled.

"Right, we typically can count on getting a whole lot of help from a suspect," the counselor snipped.

The pair didn't wait for permission. The sheriff was already familiar with the barn. The dogs were familiar with him, too. They sniffed after him with their wet noses.

The counselor wandered into the shadows of the barn. He looked at the tack room and down shed row. He walked back out the door and into the sunlight. The sheriff stayed behind, like the maneuver was planned.

"What's going on out here? Where's the Greeley girl? We know it was Henry, and we know you know all about it," the sheriff said, as the counselor stepped back inside the barn. "Go on back outside, counselor. Let's let this be a private conversation. I think I can get through to him."

The counselor, a stern man, pushed the brim of his black Stetson up to his hairline and left the barn. The sheriff turned back to me. He wasn't cheerful, and he no longer used the churlish bumbling as a pretext.

"You don't want to get into a pissing match with the lawyers over this. It just ain't smart. They got too many ways to hurt a smarty pants who thinks he can get away with withholding information on a minor. That Greeley girl is missing, and she is a minor. That's serious business you don't want to be no part of. That's kidnapping."

"I'd tell you something if I knew something."

"It might keep Henry out of jail. He was over to Ballston Spa that night the Greeley girl was kidnapped. You know where else we tracked him?"

"No. Where?"

"Here. That's why we're here. I am not calling you a liar. I am telling you to avoid a pissing match with these lawyers. They got too many ways to hurt you, even if you're innocent. They might even charge you with a conspiracy to commit kidnapping."

"How so?"

The Horse

"I don't exactly know how so. I only know the so part. Lawyers can charge you without information, and they can make your life miserable from there. You'll appear before Judge Hulbert, which ain't going to be pretty, and you'll end up in the jail until they sort things out, which ain't going to be pretty either. Kidnapping is serious business, and we ain't even got to what happened to Mr. Tripps's horse yet."

I already knew the answer to how things would work out for me, of course. It didn't require me to consult the Evil Man. Judge Hulbert and Gerrit Smith, attorney and counselor-at-law, were likely good friends with Mr. Tripps and even better friends with Mr. Tripps's money. I didn't need clarification on what was likely to happen to Henry, a colored groom. He wasn't likely to survive a lynch mob, unless he made it across the northern border. I put my hands in my pockets and looked at the dogs. I took my hands out of my pockets just long enough to pet them, which was a way of buying time to think of a clever response.

"A little nervous, aren't you?"

"You'd be a little nervous, too, if the tables were turned."

"If I was a horse trainer, and I had clients, I might have taken a little better care of that filly than to let her just walk off like that, you know what I mean?" he asked, not expecting an answer. "I might also have decided it was a good idea to side with the law instead of a groom who couldn't keep his pants buttoned. You know, of the ten things that can happen to a fellow when he decides to unbutton his pants, nine of them are bad. And kidnapping ain't even on the bad list. Kidnapping is so bad it's got a list all of its very own."

"Kidnapping? Henry?"

"We've been out to see the girl's parents. They didn't give her permission to leave the farm. She's a minor. That makes it an open and shut case of kidnapping. I got the paperwork on my desk. I got to do something about it."

"My guess would be that Henry got scared and tried to do the noble thing. I don't know for sure why, sheriff, no more than I know for sure why you and that lawyer out there acting like I committed some kind of crime. Maybe if her parents were paying closer attention to her she wouldn't have found the opportunity to get herself knocked up like that."

"Hush up the vulgarity. We are talking about a girl here."

"Girl. Some of these girls have a way of looking womanly, and good parents keep an eye on the process

The Horse

while it is underway. I know nothing about where their daughter is. She ain't here. I can tell you that."

The churlish routine returned. He took out a little pad and wrote out a note. "You don't know what happened to that filly either, right? When's the last time you saw the filly anyway?"

"I don't recall."

"Hmmm, you don't recall."

"Nope."

"You hear from Henry, you tell that darkie to get that girl back here and stay away from her from there. Good news is we can't arrest you for it, and we can't arrest you for the filly, not yet anyway."

"No," I said grimly, "you ain't got no case against me because there ain't no case to get."

"But," he said, putting away the note pad, "There's time to get one together. The lawyers told me which way this is going to go. Good day."

He walked out of the barn. I didn't follow him. He stopped to pet one of the dogs. I felt betrayed. The dogs could at least have sensed the sheriff was the enemy of the hand that fed them. They could have growled, barked, snarled, anything. Instead, they wagged their tails and lolled their tongues. It was my time to remain silent. I was relieved the dogs couldn't talk. They witnessed the whole story. If caught, I hoped Henry wouldn't give me up. Better yet, I hoped Henry could pull it off and make it across the border.

****

Many days went by without another visit. The fall was doing the work of staining the hillsides with the colors orange, yellow, and red. I had plenty of chores around the barn to keep my mind off Henry. The horses weren't going to ever make it to the races, but they constantly needed feeding, walking, and clean stalls. I began reading the New Testament. That certainly didn't help. The stories written on the pages seemed to taunt me. The taunts came more rapidly and in single words. Arrest. Kidnapping. Conspiracy. Larceny.

****

One night about a week after the sheriff's last visit, I sat on the upholstered wing chair in the tack room reading the New Testament with my back to the door, deep in thought. I saw the connections everywhere between the parables and the Evil Man. If I didn't know better, I'd have sworn the New Testament was written with the Evil Man in mind.

The filly crept up to the tack room, tossed her head about, and silently nudged open the door with her

The Horse

muzzle. The filly poked her face across the room close enough to me to innocently sniff my shoulder blades with her curiously dry and wide-open nostrils.

I dropped the New Testament on the tack pile, screamed, and jumped to my feet. When I did, the filly tossed her head vigorously. She used her muzzle to nudge me more forcibly, throwing me backward into the upholstered chair. The force nearly threw the chair over. I laughed irrationally, and instead of confronting the filly, I stooped to pick up the book. When I righted myself, Lizzie W was gone.

I saw the rafters overhead. There was water dripping. I had no idea where it was coming from. It was strange that it hadn't rained in days, yet there was water. Then, the drops became a steady stream. I wondered how much of it would come down.

I swung out of the tack room looking for the filly. The filly wasn't on shed row. The barn door was open. There was a draft. I walked slowly, very slowly, toward the open door. The filly wasn't there. Next, I checked the gravesite. The hay had disappeared. The hole was not left open like an enormous cavity in a molar. Instead, it was a polite hole, evenly spaced, purposely left open. The filly was no longer here.

I thought of a passage from Leviticus: *Both of them have committed an abomination; they shall be put to death.* I looked slyly at the open barn door. Had Lizzie W come to life with the raccoons? *Was the Evil Man in on this?* I told myself to stop thinking, to stop coming up with weird suppositions. *If the filly lives, what happened to the hole in the back of her head. Did it heal? Does she seek revenge?* I convinced myself that I couldn't revoke the laws of gravity or reason to come up with a plausible explanation. The only solution was to convince myself that none of this happened, that it was all a nightmare. The sheriff, the prosecutor, Henry, the Greeley girl, Lizzie W, all of them, were only part of a nightmare, a prank. I might wake up from all of it.

I vigorously and desperately filled in the hole with everything I had at my disposal, which were my bare hands and boots. I sweated profusely as I moved the piles of earth and smoothed over the gravesite. I kicked hay over what had been the gravesite, so that it resembled a disheveled child.

I went to the tack room and found one of Henry's whiskey bottles and threw back a belt of the brown whiskey. My fingers began to tremble. I knew it would be foolish to flee. It would be taken as an admission of guilt. Only the guilty flee. I amended the thought: Only the guilty and the persecuted flee, huge distinction.

Unlike a colored groom, I wasn't among the persecuted. I was only guilty if convicted, and the only

The Horse

evidence of guilt was the gravesite, which was now empty, and the lips of the accused, which were now sealed. If I didn't run, and I didn't talk, the odds were in my favor. The filly walked right out of the barn and into the wind. It was a relief the evidence was no longer within my constructive possession.

This left the issue of the dripping water. I returned to the tack room and looked to the rafters. I could fix a leak on my own. The typical way was to replace shingles on the roof. Water not only seeks its own level, it warps roofs, finds openings and runs to spots where it can drip free. In other words, it doesn't necessarily mean the breach is at the spot where it leaks.

I needed work capable of punishing me, making me too tired to give my circumstances much, if any, thought by day, and I had the whiskey and the New Testament to occupy my mind at night. Sometimes hard work is the only elixir, the only answer.

The next day I rode into town looking for roofing shingles. I had some of the gambling proceeds in my pocket. My horse loped leisurely along. I tipped my Stetson whenever I saw a lady wearing an elaborate hat. If the sheriff saw me, it was important that I look casual, diffident. I purchased roofing shingles, roofing nails, and a carpenter's apron. I stopped for a shot of whiskey at the Regis Hotel. I sat at the long bar and got lost in the jumpy tune a colored pianist banged out on a standup piano. I thought of what the New Testament said about salvation, the ways to sidestep our misdeeds. The Evil Man spoke to a different point of view. The Evil Man dismissed the need to apologize for anything, especially the fallibility of the flesh. Misdeeds live on forever, or as close to forever that matters. There is no escape. In the end, we are all caught. In the end, we all suffer.

****

In Syracuse that same week, a colored man wearing a red bandanna wrapped around his head and covering all but his eyes smashed the plate glass of the Syracuse Savings Bank at or near closing time. He pointed a Derringer at a pretty teller named Maureen Allyn, and demanded all the money she had in her cash box. She passed a sum of over 200 dollars, mostly in Union notes. As the colored man left the bank, he stuffed away the money in his pants, at least most of it anyway. There were a couple of notes that fell to the floor. Foolishly, he stooped to pick up the missing notes. As he faced the floor, a retired police officer working the security detail that day said: "You put all of that money back right now, boy!" That turned out to be the epitome of foolishness.

The Horse

The colored man fired the Derringer. Several customers screamed. Everyone hit the floor, including the tellers behind the bars. The officer staggered and stumbled to the floor, clutching his chest. It wasn't clear whether he had been hit or the excitement triggered a cardiac arrest.

The colored man ran out of the bank, yanking the bandanna from his face. The bank manager wearing a white shirt bravely ran into the street with his hands raised to witness the spectacle of the getaway. The colored man climbed onto the box of a coach next to a pretty young girl with a baby growing in her belly.

****

I climbed onto the roof of the barn in the midday sun dragging roofing shingles. I picked a day when the sky was empty of rain clouds. I freed old shingles on the roof with the claw of a hammer and let them fall to the ground. The grit and tar flew back at my face. With roofing nails in my mouth, I hammered away at the new shingles. The hammering echoed back at me from somewhere across the town. The work took most of the afternoon.

I went into the tack room, stripped off my sweaty shirt, and sat on the upholstered wing chair. I opened the cabinet and found one of Henry's last whiskey bottles pushed all the way toward the back of the shelf. My fingers were still a bit numb from all that hammering, but I got the top of the bottle off. I slumped back in the chair. I hated to admit it, but I had taken a liking to Henry's brown whiskey. The tack room door eased open. A raccoon with an enormous head appeared.

If I had time to think, that raccoon would never have gotten away. If I was a spiteful man, I would have crushed glass and rolled it in peanut butter and set the treat down for the critter to eat itself to death long ago. But conscious thinking had been eliminated by surprise and horror. I suppose if any man is startled by his worst nightmare, it was me. I didn't even realize I was naked from the waist up. I grabbed the hammer and went hunting raccoon. I went on tiptoe down shed row and found the raccoon in the shadows of the first empty stall I met, the one with the gravesite. I brought my right boot down on the raccoon's neck. I could feel the critter struggling to free itself. I could feel its teeth desperately gnashing against the leather of my boot. It had a good hold on my boot, and I had a good hold on its neck. I pushed even harder.

If I let even an ounce of pressure off my boot, the critter would scamper free, or worse, it might go on the attack. Watching a living being struggle against death is a great horror, but feeling it is another matter altogether. It couldn't get to me as long as I kept my foot on its neck. It used its claws and tail to climb and twist around my leg to get high enough to bite me; I could see the spaces between its sharp teeth. I slammed its head with the claw of the hammer. The critter cried. I felt the skull crack. The blood gushed, and I could feel the critter quit the struggle.

I removed my boot from its neck and commenced bludgeoning the head with the flat head of the hammer. I needed confirmation the critter was dead, dead, dead. I hammered the skull with even greater force than I hammered the roofing nails. The reason is I had a better angle on the job. I wasn't hammering against a slanted roof. I was hammering a warm pelt with both of my feet planted squarely on the earth.

The blood sprayed and squirted, but the lifeless head was no longer in the struggle. The lifeless, rotund body flopped. I hammered on. The hammering sent me into a sort of trance. I was no longer in the fight, I had entered the dream of the fight, a sort of pantomime. The same way one can be swept up into a monastic chant or the swoops and dives of a piano solo, I lost consciousness. I am not sure what church my mind was in, and I couldn't begin to name the pew, and the fact is, I wasn't even sure my mind was in a church, but

I can say a mysterious thought got stuck in my head involving a single word. Victory.

I hammered away. There was life left somewhere in the warm pelt, because the tail lashed against my calf, wrapped around it, coiled. This sent me into a frenzy. I am not sure how many blows I struck after that. There were too many to count. The blood gushed through the raccoon's mouth. Its tiny black rat eyes were left open. I was sure the creature was dead. The trance was over.

I held the raccoon up by the tail. The weight of its own disgustingly rotund body caused it to dangle and spin lifelessly. The claws were open, frozen forever. Its mouth was fixed in a battle snarl. I walked into the open air outside the barn holding the tail away from my body. I was thinking of a place to lay the carcass to rest. There was no logical place, so I slung the tail round and round. I desecrated the pelt by treating it like a stone in a sling shot and sent it sailing through the air. It came to rest in a patch of weeds a suitable distance away from the barn door. I figured the pelt might eventually draw flies and stink. If so, so much the better.

****

Oddly, I mainly remember the desecration of the pelt rather than the way I sent the claw of the hammer into the raccoon's skull. It is rather like turning the pages of a family album and looking at yellowed photographs of dead relatives. That raccoon was huge. It was easily a thirty-pounder. I wondered how they got that big, that child-like.

Then it was the same coon that had been hanging around the dead filly and the gravesite, I hear you thinking. I am sure it was. There is no way to tell one raccoon from another. The essential markings are roughly the same on all of them. The black burglar's mask about the eyes and the black rings on the gray tail don't distinguish one raccoon from another. However, there is a huge difference in size. This raccoon had an unusually large and arrogant head. That's the thing that stood out for me. I went back into the barn and wandered into the empty stall. I kicked around the hay and wondered how much the critter weighed. When I slung it into the weeds, there was a feeling of weightlessness.

Back in the tack room, I kneeled alongside the pile of tack. I began to hold up the leather straps and look at them like they were calculus problems before untangling them and laying them over a hook on the wall one by one. If you've ever worked with horses, you know you want everything organized just so. The reason is because when you get a horse ready to work and lead it out of its stall, the last thing you need is to waste time untangling the tack and run the risk of turning an otherwise calm horse into one that is suddenly fractious. These beasts can turn a hair at the drop of a pin.

I rolled up the turndowns and shin bandages and put them in a desk drawer on the right-hand side of the desk. I began pulling open the other drawers on that side of the desk, occupying my mind by scrounging around in the clutter, and saw Mr. Tripps's silks in the deep bottom drawer. I pulled out the silks, unfolded them, held them up to admire them and reflected on how they looked on the jockey as she blew by Captain Moore through the stretch of the third leg of the match race. I reverently hung them on a hook on the wall next to the tack. I kicked the drawer closed with the toe of my boot, and curiosity led me to begin to pull open the rest of the desk drawers on the left-hand side of the desk. I found the silk cap. I reunited the cap on the same hook with the silks. I sat on the upholstered chair and leaned across the desk to the bottom drawer on the left-hand side of the desk.

I pulled it open, the final drawer. A baby raccoon's head popped out of the clutter. I screamed in revulsion and fell backward. The baby fell to its back, righted itself, clawed its way over the top of the drawer, and tumbled to the floor. The critter looked like a scrawny cat, except for its mature grey tail. It stood upright, snarled, and was a grey blur as it swirled away from me and escaped out the tack room door all before I could collect my wits.

I had the good sense to grab a shovel and go hunting raccoon. Where there was a baby, the mother couldn't be far behind. I knew the mother was somewhere in the barn, and I thought if there was one baby, there were likely to be others. I tried to remember how many kits are in a typical raccoon litter, but my mind went blank.

I ran into shed row. There was no sign of the mother or her kit. The barn door was open. I went outside to look around. I saw the weeds that concealed the carcass of their fallen brother. It hadn't begun to smell. I circumambulated the barn. Nothing.

I was surprised and mildly disappointed. I thought someone might come to the barn, announce a charge in the case of the missing filly and the local pregnant girl, or at least take me into custody for questioning. I figured it would be the sheriff, the prosecutor, Mr. Greeley, or perhaps the judge himself. They didn't, though.

Instead, it was Lizzie W herself and a retinue of raccoons.

****

You're probably wondering how I knew about Henry's actions at the Syracuse First National Bank and the Syracuse Savings Bank. If you are, you've probably already wondered, *Well, a colored groom fresh from two bank robberies on the run with a pregnant girl and so far away from Canada is not a very wise enterprise given the political climate of 1863, even if the couple was smart enough to be on their way to seeking refuge on a stop on the underground railroad in Skaneateles.* You may not have the foggiest idea about what a stop on the underground railroad looked like. I didn't know myself.

I started reading the weekly newspapers, of course. Bank robberies make sensational copy. I wrote letters to people who lived in the area. I received thoughtful replies, willingly regaling me with rumors of the exploits of the duo. That sort of investigative work may intrigue you, but those rumors came to me years later, and they only confirmed what I already knew.

Already knew? you ask. Yes, already knew. I knew it before it happened. How? The answer brings us close to the crux of the matter. Lizzie W's raccoons told me. You have no way of believing such a thing. I don't blame you. That makes you rational. And I have just told you an irrational thought.

The Horse

In order to suspend disbelief, I remind you that this is a confession, my last words in this life as we know it. I am in a room at the Adelphi Hotel preparing for the eternity promised in the New Testament, so I am including only facts I know to be true. The last thing I would do is taint my confession with a falsehood or a deliberate exaggeration.

****

By the summer of 1864, Jim Morrissey had attracted a lot more business to the grounds. He switched the racetrack to the opposite side of Union Avenue to take advantage of the open space needed to meet the demands of large crowds. There were other outfits with entire strings stabled there. In the mornings, the track was busy with exercise boys jogging horses around the oval. There was a legitimate race meeting with several races a day on the card during the month of August, including two stake races featuring rather large purses.

I didn't have a single hopeful in my barn that was a serious candidate for any of that purse money. Nevertheless, I walked horses over to the track every morning. I'd find time to work at least two horses every day. There were rumors the war was winding down. Mr. Lincoln promised to reconcile all differences with the South by simply requiring Confederate sympathizers to swear out an oath to abide by the U.S. Constitution, a good deal given the massive number of casualties and the toll the war had taken on the country as a whole. This spirit of cooperation contributed to the overall sense of exuberance in a town that had already become an international destination for members of high society looking for a place to simply be rich together, given Saratoga's reputation for gaiety, endless parties, fine art, avant garde music, and the medicinal properties of its mineral spas. In short, Saratoga was bustling, and I was uniquely stationed to witness it all.

Mr. Morrissey knew that horse racing was the perfect venue for this society. I confess to slipping into town to attend a party or two. On one of those occasions I was guilty of extreme excess and public drunkenness such that I don't remember exactly how I came to retire to the safety of the tack room in the barn. I woke sprawled out on the upholstered wing chair the next night. I drank so much brown whiskey the day before that I lost track of time. I woke to the sound of horses whinnying outside the tack room and assumed the raccoons had returned. The sun was already at full mast.

I was shocked to find that all of the stalls in the barn were empty. The latches had been sprung, and the webbing was thrown aside. I ran out the barn door and

The Horse

into the sunlight searching for the horses. I didn't have to look very far. They were standing together in a herd in the paddock. At the center of the herd was the filly herself, Lizzie W. She was whinnying, pawing at the ground, preaching to the other horses that had formed something of a congregation.

"Get! You're dead! Get on!" I screamed. Lizzie W spotted me, turned away, and galloped off. It felt like a dream, but I knew it wasn't a dream.

Lizzie W didn't comply with my demand. Lizzie W playfully jumped at the air, tossed her head, and broke into a gallop. She joined the oval where jockeys were busy exercising horses. She was the riderless horse that joined the slower horses at the back of the pack. She galloped in company with those horses, snorting, eyeballing them, cajoling them, and then mysteriously veering off course.

The startled jockeys stood up in the irons, eased their mounts and looked around for the riderless horse, but Lizzie W sprinted to a gap in the rail and disappeared along the backstretch area before the jockeys had the time to believe their eyes. There was another occasion that very summer when I was out jogging a horse before sunrise and Lizzie W drew alongside. I remember the exact horse I was on, Red Cardinal. I had to take Red Cardinal out very early because she was very untalented and a threat to bolt or interfere with the works of the more legitimate racehorses at Saratoga.

The races that summer were particularly telling. In each instance, any horse that had been visited by Lizzie W, regardless of its odds or talent level, managed to prevail in its races, creating some shocking upsets of favorites that had formerly been regarded as unbeatable by the betting public. As for Red Cardinal, she won her race at the impossible odds of 90-1 over a prohibitive favorite that had been bet down to odds of 4/5. That summer Mr. Morrissey's racetrack became known as the graveyard of champions thanks to the periodic visits of Lizzie W.

I had become taken with brown whiskey that summer, too. I started throwing up the stuff in the late afternoons, which made me pass out immediately after I fed the horses in the early evening hours. If I said I only passed out, I was being polite. It is more accurate to say that on most days I blacked out until the cock crowed. During one of those violent thunderstorms that bedevil the mountains around Saratoga, I slept through the rattling and scraping noises the wind sent through the barn. The horses were quiet.

The rain swept out of the area just as quickly as it blew in, but the rattling and scraping continued. The persistence of those sounds after all was still outside the barn disturbed the period after the storm when all of nature is at peace, and it roused me from the fog of alcohol. I didn't move. I waited for a minute or so to determine whether I was actually hearing what I thought I heard. I was.

I had seen raccoons on the loose and a dead filly vacate a gravesite, so I was willing to accept the eventuality that I was delusional – I hadn't really seen any of it. I just believed I had. Then, I heard a boom that was undeniably a loud, percussive sound made against the sealed barn door. I ventured out of the tack room and rolled back the barn door. Lizzie W was standing there, ears twitching. The back of her head was still gaping wide open from the gunshot exit wound. Her eyes were red and lifeless. The brown color of glass marbles was gone. Nevertheless, her eyes seemed fixed in a stare that peered straight through me. It was a knowing stare. Why not? The dead know everything that is knowable.

The filly was surrounded by her entourage. Without them, she would be merely an ordinary ghost or worse an occupant of a shallow grave. They were her life blood. She was their queen. Her bones showed. She walked casually up to me with her signature sweeping gate that complimented her royal blood lines. The raccoons crowded around her, some looking up at her romantically, some at me with utter disgust.

The filly raised her tail, and the most abominable odor escaped as she dropped her business on the ground. She showed the wild white of her eyes and began to whinny, except the whinnying didn't sound like whinnying. Instead, it sounded like gurgling, like blood clotting in her long royal throat and forming into a glue. She raised her head and began loping toward me, and her enormous nostrils flared and worked to try to smell me, like the dogs had once worked to get a whiff of the sheriff's smelly crotch. "Leave me alone. Why are you here? You're not really here. Go away! You're dead, and you are rotting in a shallow grave."

I could smell the filly's decaying flesh as her head bobbed. The filly I had thoughtfully selected at the sales, fed, brushed, galloped, and cheered on during the heats of her match race was surrounded by her royal escort. The raccoons scampered around my feet and brushed against my calves. They, too, sniffed at my flesh. I recoiled from the approaching mob. The filly pawed at the dust, like she did when she first spied Captain Moore in the paddock.

She nudged me with her muzzle and nibbled at my shirt like I was a carrot or a cube of sugar, but

The Horse

she didn't bite. I backpedaled with mouth agape and reached for the barn door. I had the instinct to flee the mob, but I was frozen with fear. The smell of decaying flesh was overwhelming. I wretched, but didn't vomit (not yet anyway). I can see the mob now as I compose this written confession. I wanted to die back then and escape it all, but my heart was leaping around in my chest. The filly snorted, and all of the dead, putrid air in her lung sacs exploded in a cloudy mist that smelled like one thousand dead raccoons. I belched and vomited into my hands.

The horse grunted as if to tell me the things only the dead could possibly know. I screamed. I promised to kill myself if only the filly would stop. But the filly didn't stop. She couldn't. The dead don't show mercy. Mercy is only relevant to the living.

I know that now.

****

After slapping the horses and fleeing the Syracuse Savings Bank, Henry sought refuge for his "wife" in a community of Quakers in the tiny Village of Skaneateles, which probably felt like heaven for the expectant parents, but actually was a dank basement of a grand white house, quite possibly the absolute last place on earth you'd expect them to "lay low." The village in the Finger Lakes near the Canadian border is a place where people enjoyed being rich together. The Quakers took this as the perfect cover for a stop on the Underground Railroad. For those who don't know history, the Underground Railroad was a secret network of safe houses where fugitive slaves, often led by Harriet Tubman and other similarly courageous souls, took solace while on perilous missions to "steal away" to freedom in the North.

The Greeley girl was not a fugitive slave, but she might as well have been one. She was a young lady who was in trouble and in labor in one of the upstairs bedrooms of the safe house. She was only thirteen-years-old at the time. The Quakers had separated her from Henry who was cowering and waiting in the dank basement with over 200 dollars stuffed in his pocket, the same basement where fugitive slaves once cowered and waited for the opportunity to resume their missions to evade slave catchers, U.S. marshals, and other mobs in the race to freedom. I confess to saying this with a measure of pride and affection. I figured he'd have gotten lynched immediately after he robbed the bank, but he proved me wrong. He was in love, he was scared, he was on the run, he was still burdened by the guilty conscience that he and I had destroyed the filly in the most horrific way, but in spite of all of that, Henry

The Horse

demonstrated bravery and resourcefulness to spirit his "wife" to safety, even if the safety was only temporary. I am still sad that I led him to stain his soul with the act of cruelty we visited upon a defenseless horse, a creature of nature, and I led him to this fate, like a pony with a brass shank tied to its bridle.

Henry was relegated to the basement hideout while the birthing process was underway upstairs. At the time, I wasn't aware exactly where the safe house was located, but I later learned it was opposite the grey stone markers of an increasingly crowded cemetery down the road from the City of Auburn.

In Auburn, there were intellectuals and politicians of note everywhere, including abolitionists. There were grand houses with majestic gables and vast barren open land. It was perfect ground for civil war skirmishes and hideouts. Henry, fresh from robbing two banks, couldn't afford to be seen outside during daylight hours. He needed a hideout.

A foolish man would have ventured outside and been snared by the marshals or a lynch mob. Henry was smarter than that. He "laid low." He adapted to life in a hideout, watched the sunlight play on the dust particles beneath the cellar windows and wondered how life with a baby and a "wife" would change him.

The trouble didn't end there. The child was stillborn, and of course the Greeley girl didn't blame the Quaker midwife, her tender years, or anything of the sort. She blamed Henry, and she did so at the top of her lungs.

Quite possibly, the time she spent birthing made her lose her mind, or it might have happened at the Syracuse First National Bank or the Syracuse Savings Bank. She insisted upon an ice cream soda, and she demanded that Henry go into the world to get it. She didn't care about anything in the entire world apart from that ice cream soda, and that included Henry. A colored man exiting a grand house in Skaneateles, New York in 1864 had a way of attracting curiosity, and curiosity swiftly came to the attention of the authorities.

This coincided with Henry's journey past the lakefront, under street lamps and onward to a storefront bakery. He correctly assumed the bakery had many of the delights that would soften the blue mood of a teenage girl, including ice cream soda. The teenage girls attending the glass counter flirted with Henry while they leaned into ice cream scoops to dig ice cream out of vats. Each time the girl pawed at the bottom of a vat her blouse exposed the lion's share of her upright bosom flopping and swaying. She unexpectedly stopped and caught a spellbound Henry perhaps a bit too eager to purchase scoops of ice cream, ice cream soda, or practically anything else that was for sale in the tiny bakery. This placed his propensity squarely on display.

Henry, the same colored groom who had consorted with an underaged girl in Saratoga, a girl who at this very moment was in recovery from the turmoil of a stillbirth, agreed to wait for the girl on a bench outside of the bakery. Henry leaned against a brick wall and read a newspaper. After a while, he saw a cigar butt on the ground and got the idea to stoop to pick it up. He figured he might be able to get it lit and take a draw of blue smoke off what was left of it while he waited. This caused him to overlook a team pulling a wagon load of exactly three hicks, one small boy, and one basset hound. The wagon came to a halt on the opposite side of the street. The men hopped off the wagon and wandered over to Henry.

"You staying up the road there with them Quakers, boy?" An older man with a grey circle goatee urged Henry from his daydream.

At that instant, Henry heard the sound of the iron links of a chain being dragged out of the back of the wagon. He couldn't fix upon fine detail in the commotion, but the sound the chain made was unmistakable. The pack didn't rough him up. They didn't have to. He was fully compliant.

Through the haze of the commotion, he wasn't likely to identify a single one of the faces of any of the men or the boy in the pack, the boy with the freckled, toothy face, the chubby man, or any of them, even if he was later asked to do so by the authorities. However, he did manage to focus on the one older man standing alone on the wagon bed. While there was commotion and insults on the ground, the man on the wagon bed calmly looked down on the proceedings without moving at all. Henry didn't know what to think or how to interpret the calm demeanor of this man who remained fixed in the air above the proceedings like a statue. Was he friendly? Would he intervene on his behalf and call the whole thing off? The passersby were perfectly indifferent. That needed no interpretation.

The man on the wagon bed had a clubfoot. Henry saw the foot through the open end of the wagon, and then he heard his deformity slapping and dragging against the wagon bed as the man struggled to free a knot or a tangle out of the last few feet of the chain's length. Henry wanted to believe the older man would show mercy. However, there was no mercy. There was only the face of pure meanness and the sound of the chain links and the man's deformity slapping and dragging against the bed of the wagon. Henry figured his life had only another five minutes or so to run. He was right.

As soon as the men got the chain, they pushed him dismissively into the wagon and proceeded to the shadows of the nearby wooded area, dragging the chain along the ground behind them as they went like a snake. They found a tree with a suitable trunk. The tree looked familiar to Henry, but he wasn't sure why. The men pressed his body flat against the trunk. The man with the club foot expertly wrapped the full length of the chain around Henry and the trunk again and over again. He stopped to give the chain a yank to make it tight, and then he kept fussing with the chain to make it rest just so against his rib cage.

Henry's entire pectoral girdle heaved with adrenalin. The pack was suddenly quiet as the men, and the boy, waited for something to happen. The man with the club foot kept working and adjusting and admiring and tightening the chain. The chain was ever so tight. Henry's body couldn't accept any more pressure. Nevertheless, the man didn't stop. He threw even more of his weight and might against the chain.

"I'll never forget you cowards," Henry declared in a whisper, preparing to use his final breath to curse the devils.

Henry's bones snapped. The chain was pulled so tight he could no longer figure out how to breathe. His mouth dropped open. This made the men howl with delight.

The boy did not laugh. He was quiet with horror and disbelief. He only stared. It must have been his first time.

Henry squirmed against the chain briefly and then belched. He could taste the blood in his mouth. The last thing he tasted before the final darkness that comes to us all, colored and white alike, was that blood in his throat. Henry's life as a fugitive had ended.

All of these things came to me in a dream while the raccoons prowled and the filly began to stink from the gaping wound at the back of her head. I wanted to die and join Henry where I was convinced he had taken up residence in the afterlife. I confess to not being absolutely sure about what, if anything, happens in the afterlife, or even whether there is an afterlife. One can only hope. Like practically everyone, I had learned that the wages of sin are death, but I forgot the rest of it, the part that pertains to the afterlife. Nevertheless, there were things I can report with absolute certainty. A nation torn by civil war is unlikely to anger over the fate of a dead horse or a colored groom. But revenge is quite another matter altogether, isn't it?

The Horse

****

It may have been the second or third day of the race meeting when I received a visitor at the barn. I was absolutely sure of it. I only had to take two short steps into the sunlight outside the rear barn door.

Lizzie W stood in the paddock. She was staring back at the barn door, waiting. She was sporting a bridle, the hardware of a humbled beast. The exit wound at the back of her head had not only healed. It had disappeared.

I am not sure how a ghost gets a bridle, but that was indisputably the case. The filly had extricated Blood Moon from its stall. The filly was good at unhooking the web latches at the door of the stalls. Lizzie W seemed to dare me to intervene. She stared at me, cocked her head, twitched her ears, tossed her head, and then seemed to look past me or maybe even through me.

Blue Moon was a seven-year-old race mare that had been entered in the first race on that day's race card. The filly was nudging the old nag, snorting and pawing. It was as if the filly was imploring Blood Moon to rise up and compete. I felt that if this was a conspiracy, it was a conspiracy for naught. The reason is Blood Moon had an unblemished record of never bothering to lift a single foot to race competitively on any of her previous ten starts. She didn't have a competitive bone in her body. I even question whether she had the bloodlines to qualify as a racehorse. To put it politely, Blood Moon was a hopeless longshot. It was in against a champion race mare in the first race. Typically, every race run over the Saratoga trotting course features a champion from one of the tracks in Louisiana, Texas or Kentucky. Today's first race was not an exception.

And another thing about the ghost, the full fury of Lizzie W's weight and fitness had been restored. The muscles under her dappled coat were unmistakably vigorous. She looked more like an athletic colt than a filly. She stamped and tossed her head. The brass links on the bridle sang out. She snorted like she did when we saddled her in the paddock for the Captain Moore race. I guess I had replaced Captain Moore as her primary competition.

The ghost looked at me until it was confident I had made eye contact, and then she turned her head away and galloped off. I gathered up the nag and returned it to the barn.

****

I threw the boy up into the saddle, and Blood Moon pranced off to the post parade on the grass course.

The Horse

The trumpet blared. The sky-blue silks and white cap seemed to glow in the sunlight. The other horses in the parade danced, too. Blood Moon had been dismissed by the bettors. It was an impossible longshot going off at the lusty odds of 45-1.

The horses lined up at the starter's rope. Several of the horses were slick with sweat. Others were nervous. One of the horses was fractious and even reared before settling down. This didn't delay the start. The boy dropped the rope, and the race was on.

Blood Moon went to lead like she was shot out of a canon. She opened up a three-length lead on the field. As they raced past the stands and around the first turn, the bettors assumed Blood Moon would tire and fade, and the race would develop along the backstretch. The favored horses, including the champion race mare, would run past Blue Moon as was typical of horses that went roaring along on early leads.

Blood Moon ran at least two paths away from the rail along the backstretch. Therefore, there was plenty of space between Blood Moon and the rail. Any of her competitors had plenty of space to mount a challenge along the rail, and the field could also decide to circle wide around Blood Moon. There was no such challenge. Blood Moon remained in control of the pace.

The bettors and probably the jockeys believed that Blue Moon would collapse on the lead. They probably believed the fractions were too fast for Blood Moon to remain on the lead over a distance of ground. They probably believed Blood Moon was cheap speed, and perhaps she was.

I was amazed that Blood Moon had run at all, but run she did. The crowd roared as the field turned for home. The bettors implored the horses they backed to run down Blood Moon. However, Blood Moon was not tiring. On the contrary, Blood Moon laid out and opened up. The bettors waited for a challenge. The bettors believed there would be a challenge. No such challenge came. Blood Moon hit the finish line first scoring by at least four lengths at odds of 45-1.

A stony silence fell over the crowd. I was silent, too. Those odds would have made me a very rich man if only I had the foresight to lay a bet. I didn't. I had no more idea Blood Moon would win than anyone else. Actually, I would have been the least likely person to bet on that horse. The reason: I knew the horse.

As I posed for the win photograph, I thought of the ghost, Lizzie W. I knew she had something to do with this aberration. I was sure of it.

The next race was the ultimate test of the champion. I didn't have an entry, so I stood watching around a crowd of bowlers. Lingering at the back of the post parade alongside a hopeless longshot, I thought I saw the filly. I rubbed my eyes. Was it true? She stopped at the sight of me, her head shot up, she stared, and her ears twitched like a cautious rabbit. I couldn't believe my eyes. She was ridden by Henry! Henry, you were lynched. You're dead! I know I betrayed you, but it's over now. You're dead!

They raced near the back of the pack. They picked up the pace alongside a hopeless longshot. The tandem closed and were the first to hit the finish line.

****

It might have been four hours after the race when I received a visitor at the barn. I had already had at the whiskey in the tack room. The horses were fed. The webbing latches before their stall doors were hooked. The barn doors were closed. All was right with the world.

The whiskey and the muted elation of the horse hitting the line first earlier in the day (muted because I didn't make a penny with the bookies) made me a bit careless, but not reckless and certainly not outwardly drunken. Still, I staggered to the barn door when the pounding on it commenced. Part of me thought it might be a trainer from a rival string or an exuberant well-wisher ready to offer congratulations or even an owner willing to offer new business in light of the surprising victory, because part of me dared to invite the delusion that I had a future as a trainer and my soul would ultimately be spared the consequences of my crime.

It was the sheriff. I got weak at the knees when I saw him, and I bent forward. If he hadn't unholstered his big gun, I might have let loose a stream of vomit at his feet. The sight of the big gun had the sobering influence to bring my innards out of turmoil. I tried to tell him I had no idea of what became of Henry or the Greeley girl, and if I had a notion they would disappear, I would have gladly alerted the authorities. However, all of that came out in a slurred garble, but the sheriff heard the names.

"They run off alright, but the boys in Skaneateles got to him before we could," the sheriff said. "But I am wondering, or should I say folks are wondering, how exactly you got that nag of yours to win that race today."

"Oh, that."

"Folks are poking around the judge wondering out loud how you got that impossible horse to win that impossible race over an impossible to beat champion."

"If you only knew..."

"Excuse me?"

"Nice win."

The Horse

"Nice win! Impossible win, and I don't believe in impossibility. Folks are calling that particular race the graveyard of a champion."

If they only knew how right they are, I thought. "Hadn't heard that one."

"I'll bet. You know, I find myself coming out here to visit you again. I think that's a pattern of some kind. Not sure what it means, but it's a pattern. I got to get to the bottom of patterns. You want to help me figure it out?"

"I don't know what you mean."

"Oh, you know exactly what I mean. There's mystery here. Where's there's mystery, there's likely to be an explanation, and the explanation usually leads to a crime of some kind. First, you had an expensive horse just vanished in thin air out here. Then, the Greeley girl disappeared. Well, we know what happened to her boyfriend as a result. Now this, a horse that never ran one day of its life suddenly goes to Jim Morrissey's racetrack and runs faster than the wind not to mention outruns a championship certified blue blood colt out of Lexington. That's too much mystery coming out of one barn for my taste, sir. There's a pattern."

"Sheriff, it sure looks—"

He cut me off. He thought I'd only lie, and why not? I had lied on each of his other visits. He couldn't prove it, but he knew it. The truth has a certain ring when you hear it, even if it comes from the witness box of a courtroom, and that bell had not been hammered by me, not by a long shot. It hadn't even been tapped, and the sheriff may not have been a criminologist, but he wasn't tone deaf either.

"When we figure out the pattern, and we will figure it out, it ain't gonna be pretty. Good day, sir." He swung his leg over his mount, pulled the reins to turn the horse's head away, and galloped off.

He had done it again. He had haunted me with what he didn't say, which was possibly worse than anything he could have said. Innuendo is the worse form of torture. It seeps into the subconscious mind, makes itself at home there, and hangs around until it is finished with you.

"Dead," I mumbled.

If I had told him the truth about killing the filly, stress would have flooded out of my mind, like air let out of a balloon, and oh, the relief. Sure, the sheriff would have held his big gun to my temple and hauled me off to the jail downtown. He would have hitched up his pants and gloated to the locals about capturing me as though I was a prized silver cup issued to the winning connections of a prestigious stakes race. But if I ended the torture by resorting to the truth, I figured I could appeal to

The Horse

the mercy of a judge and jury for my fate with a clear conscience, given that the act of killing the filly wasn't murder. A horse is merely personal property and nothing more. It is not a human being. Thusly, the death of the filly was merely an act of grand larceny, and I had an ownership stake in the horse, so in effect I had destroyed part of my own property. This was an evidentiary matter. Furthermore, I had a perfectly legitimate mitigating factor to present in my defense, given Mr. Tripps's arrogance. I played out the trial in my mind and got to the part where I was required to rely on the legitimacy of the judicial process for a fair and just application of the rule of law, a mouthful. Then I passed out.

When I woke up, I was tipped back in the upholstered wing chair in the tack room. I couldn't recall how I got there, but I knew relying on a broken judicial process for justice was childish and even bizarre. I vowed to never expose my fate to the likes of the sheriff or Judge Hulbert. Then I heard scratching at the closed barn door.

****

It would do no good to ignore the scratching at the barn door that had become hammering. If the sheriff wanted me badly enough, he could simply kick in the door. I rolled back the door, expecting the worst.

It was the Greeley girl. She was alone. I invited her inside, but wisely left the door open. The ribbons of sunlight threw shadows across shed row.

"The baby was stillborn," she volunteered, looking at the dirt on the barn floor like it contained a script. She possessed the kind of silky beauty of a woman touched by the elation and victory of motherhood.

"I am so sorry."

"No need for sorrow. I don't feel like a failure. I feel relieved actually, as bad as that sounds."

"I heard about Henry."

"So sad, the whole thing…"

I could think of absolutely nothing intelligent to add, so I walked down shed row with the girl. "Got a winner over the track the other day, a miracle win."

"That's nice…." We browsed, like we were buying horses that day. "And another thing," she added.

"What."

"You are the dead baby's father," she confided. "It was not Henry. It was you. The baby had green eyes, your eyes."

The girl said the baby had green eyes, the color of an agitated sea. She didn't quite know why she thought the child's eyes looked like the sea. She had never seen the sea. The idea just sort of jumped free in her mind.

The Horse

"The baby *is* yours," she repeated, almost as though she was debating the issue with herself. "She *has* your eyes…"

I stared. But I didn't correct her use of the present tense. How could I? I had seen a dead horse visit my barn.

My childhood habit of staring in times of trouble returned. I swear. I was a child again, a child concerned with childish things.

We did indeed have a dirty little secret we kept between us. She had appeared at the tack room alone exactly once. She was ripe and swollen and not yet a teenager at the time. She liked drawing that imaginary line from her puckered lips, between her bosom, and down her belly to the point where her fingertips stopped between her legs. The line she drew for Henry was the same line she drew for me. However, it didn't defeat me. Unlike Henry, I had full command of my proclivities.

The color green filled my mind. I imagined the Greely girl holding the baby proudly in both arms, swinging the baby around, and proudly pulling back the blanket that swaddled it.

"The baby was yours," the Greely girl persisted, switching to the past tense and staring at the dirt on shed row. "She had your eyes…"

I stared, too, but I can tell you that I no longer saw the Greely girl. I swear. I was a child again, a child concerned with childish things. My childhood habit of staring in times of trouble had returned.

I saw the night the Greely girl attempted to seduce me in the tack room. The scene of indiscretion and guilt and carnal lust played back in my mind, like a flood that overwhelms useless flat land. I was seated on the upholstered wing chair in the tack room with the Greeley girl straddling me much like Miss Heath would later straddle me, and I hesitate to belabor how we got to that point, and the how may very well not be terribly relevant. In this state, she took command and tried to make the unmentionable happen between us without even looking at me. She looked past me, like Mr. Tripps had looked past me. She wasn't clumsy or shy. She was in a hurry, like she knew where she had to go and was in a race to get there before an imaginary intruder had a chance to appear, scold her, and break it up. I resisted.

She was good at overcoming resistance. That's how I surmised she was used to it. I tensed up and fought her away with my hands and arms, and I never let my mouth get involved in the act of accepting criminal perversion. Most of me lusted after this

The Horse

moment, but part of me already had begun to regret it. Those instincts had nothing to do with what was happening on that chair. That had a momentum all of its own. I only knew that to yield to temptation would require that I also accept the full wrath of the law for the crime, and it was a crime. I did not touch that girl for the purpose of sexual gratification. I swear.

"The baby was yours!" She started sobbing uncontrollably.

"Now, we both know that is a factual impossibility, don't we?"

"Yes!" The sobbing became inconsolable.

"That baby wasn't Henry's baby either, was it?"

"No!"

"Whose was it?"

"I feel horrible! He died for that baby! And it wasn't his! This was all my fault!" I didn't want to tell her the truth. It wasn't her fault. It was Henry's fault. The Evil Man didn't feel sorry for Henry, not in the least. Henry was a fallen man, a man with extraordinary proclivities. In the proclivity department, he managed to up the ante. He fraternized with an underage white girl in the middle of a civil war. Then, he spirited her away on a fool's errand. The Evil Man took delight in watching Henry run afoul of the admonitions published practically everywhere in the Old Testament.

"If I had to guess, I'd say the baby belonged to that Crumley boy, your school chum, the one with the pimples. But that's only a wild guess. How exactly can we be sure the baby didn't belong to Henry?"

"The baby was white. That's why."

"So."

"So! What do you mean by so? Henry was black."

The Evil Man refused to let her get away with that one

"So, you ask?" I teased. "Because there are plenty of people parading around here -- masquerading around I should say -- as if they're white who are actually black. The reason I said that is to inform you that just because a baby is white doesn't mean the father ain't black or the grandfather ain't black. A white baby might very well have had a black father. It wouldn't have been the first."

"The baby had red hair."

"Now, we're getting somewhere. Henry didn't have no red hair. That baby didn't belong to Henry. No way."

"No way."

"Do you think it's the Crumley boy's?"

"I don't know."

The Horse

Those three words, "I don't know," confirmed everything I already knew about the world.

****

I heard galloping hooves outside the barn. I rolled back the barn door. It was the sheriff.

I watched him pull up his mount, clutch the saddle horn, and drag his leg over the saddle. The big gun on his hip showed before his boots landed on the ground.

"This time it ain't no dress rehearsal. I'm taking you in," he said, looking over his belly at the ground.

"You're doing what?"

"Taking you in. Got to. Judge says." He reached down to pat one of the dogs.

"Taking me in where? For what?"

The sheriff pulled his braces with his thumbs to make more room to breathe. Then, he pulled his thumbs free and let the braces snap back into place. "You know what this is about," he said. "I'm taking you in for stealing that horse, grand larceny."

"How do you steal your own horse, Sheriff?"

"You'll have plenty of time to make your points to the judge. But I gotta take you in. You've been a gentleman to me. You let us search the barn without no paperwork. Course, I ain't real sure about how innocent you are, but I got to treat you like you're innocent until the judge says otherwise. But the judge ain't got no say on how I take you in. I get to decide that. I ain't using no chains or nothing on you. You get to walk over there to see the judge like a man, hear? There'll be no chains, no spectacle. Of course, they'll be plenty of chains in jail where you'll sit until there's a trial, but I am taking you in as a man."

"Great. One step above slave catching."

"I suppose you can look at it that way. I wish you wouldn't though. By the way, ain't no slave catching anymore neither, ain't legal no more."

****

On the first day of the bench trial, the prosecutor, Gerrit Smith, Esq., called Mr. Charles Ogden Tripps as his first witness.

The air reeked of Mr. Tripps's Hour d'et Homme cologne as he took the stand. The courtroom was unlit, except for the sunlight filtering through long cathedral windows. Sunlight played against the courtroom's domed ceiling and across the empty jury box.

Judge Hulbert blinked back any hint of emotion. His shoulders were stiffly erect, like a still life painting. I would have thought the judge was impartial if I didn't know better.

The Horse

The gallery was empty, and I didn't have the money, or inclination, to hire a lawyer, so I sat at the defense table alone. There was nobody else in the courtroom to break the silence. Oddly, Judge Hulbert brought the gavel down hard on a wooden block anyway.

"Did you attend the Lexington auction where Lizzie W was sold to the highest bidder?" Smith opened the direct examination, theatrically sweeping his hand through the air.

"The Lexington Tattersall's Select Horse Auction, yes," Mr. Tripps replied, editing the question.

"What happened?"

"You may lead the witness," Judge Hulbert interjected.

"Mr. Tripps, you purchased Lizzie W, the horse that is the subject of these proceedings, with the winning bid, didn't you?" Smith continued.

"Yes, I did."

"Did you have a partner?"

"Yes, the defendant was my partner," Mr. Tripps said, pointing toward me at the defense table.

"Let the record reflect that the witness has identified the defendant."

"Yes, so noted," Judge Hulbert confirmed.

"Now, did there come a time when an ownership change occurred subsequent to that date?"

"Yes, sir."

"When?"

"On June 15, 1863, a couple of months before Lizzie W raced. The filly raced at the Saratoga trotting course on August 3, 1863. Ownership changed prior to that date. Ownership changed on June 15, 1863."

"Tell the court in what way ownership of the filly changed on June 15, 1863?"

"The defendant divested his entire ownership interest to me, and I became the sole owner."

"Did the defendant divest his ownership interest in writing?"

"Yes, in writing."

"Do you have the writing that memorialized the transaction in court today, sir?"

"Yes."

"Your honor, I'd like to offer the document that memorialized the transaction, a document which consists of a single handwritten page, as the people's exhibit one, and move its admission." Mr. Smith said, pulling the document out of the open valise on the prosecutor's table and waving it in the air, like it was a pennant.

"So ordered," said Judge Hulbert.

"May I approach the witness, your honor?"

"Yes."

"I am showing you what's been marked people's exhibit one in evidence and ask you to examine it," the attorney said, approaching the witness. "This is the original writing, correct?"

"Yes, this is it," said Mr. Tripps, reading the document.

"Is it dated?"

"Yes."

"What is the date?"

"June 15, 1863."

"Is there a signature at the end of the document?"

"Yes, the defendant signed it on the signature blank."

"And is this document in the same condition today as it was on the day it was signed?"

"Yes, it is."

"Very well. Now, subsequent to June 15, 1863, who was entrusted with the custody and control of the filly pursuant to the terms and conditions stated on this document?"

"Yes, the defendant, the horse's trainer."

"And was the filly placed in the defendant's exclusive custody and control at this time, that is, June 15, 1863?"

"Yes."

"And at all relevant times thereafter?"

"Yes."

"Objection," I said in a loud and clear voice.

I thought this seemed like the right time to object, but I wasn't sure. I didn't pretend to know the rules of evidence. As I've said, I didn't have the money, or patience, to hire a lawyer. Heck, I believed I needed a magician rather than a lawyer to get me out of this mess.

"What's your objection?" The judge prompted me to exercise the appropriate degree of decorum by motioning for me to rise to my feet prior to addressing the court further. I complied.

I didn't know what to say, so I just stood there and stared.

"Overruled. You are a layperson, so I will exercise the simple courtesy of stating the grounds for the ruling. Counselor is laying a foundation for what in the law is called a *res ipsa loquitur* case. This common law doctrine provides that if the prosecution establishes the horse was in your exclusive custody and control at all relevant times, there is a rebuttable presumption at least in civil proceedings that you are solely responsible for what happened to the filly without further proof. Now, this being a criminal proceeding and not a civil proceeding, a more exalted standard of proof applies here than in civil proceedings. Although res ipsa evidence is circumstantial evidence, and the more exalted criminal standard applies in these proceedings, which is proof beyond a reasonable doubt, and furthermore please know that I am specifically not ruling that the civil law rebuttable presumption or the *res ipsa loquitur* doctrine even applies here. The doctrine doesn't apply in criminal cases, and I am not applying in your case; however, I am ruling that circumstantial evidence in the nature of *res ipsa* evidence is generally admissible in criminal proceedings, and I am ruling that it is admissible in the case being brought against you. And this circumstantial evidence may open the door to a ruling, after the court weighs all of the evidence of record, evaluates the reliability of that evidence, and assesses the credibility of the witnesses, that I may indeed find that a reasonable inference may be drawn from circumstantial evidence sufficient to support a finding that you are guilty as charged. Is that clear?"

It was clear that I was getting screwed.

"Your honor, may I look at the document?" I was still standing upright, careful not to shift my weight or walk in place, thank God. I figured nervous energy of any kind might make me appear guilty. I also wasn't sure if I needed to ask for permission to sit back down.

Mr. Smith didn't wait for a ruling. He shuffled across the courtroom, disgustingly dropped the document on the defense table without bothering to look directly at me, and arrogantly strolled back to the prosecution's table without comment. I eagerly lifted the document up to the light.

"What on earth are you doing?" Judge Hulbert asked. Deep furrows invaded his forehead.

"I am looking at the document," I said curtly, not bothering to look away from the document to explain myself further. I turned toward the long cathedral windows and held the document up toward the sunlight.

"We know you are looking at the document. The question is what are you doing?" Mr. Smith said.

The thoughts streaming through my mind stumbled over Mr. Smith's use of the word *we*. However, I kept my composure. I didn't take my eyes off of that document. "I am looking for the truth," I mumbled.

"And you expect to find it like that, looking up at the ceiling?" The court inquired.

"I need the light."

"Well," Judge Hulbert chuckled. "Don't we all need the light? But what on earth... Never mind, take your time. Go ahead."

"What do you call this?" Mr. Smith asked.

"Counselor, I'd call this a criminal defendant who is unrepresented by counsel, is what I'd call it. No, we will let him have all the time he requires to, as he puts it, to find the truth."

The Horse

And so, I did. I took my time. I held Mr. Tripps's writing up to the sunlight streaming through the long cathedral windows. I should say I looked straight through that writing, like it was a window or a specimen magnified under a microscope, and I kept it up to that light for what seemed like an eternity.

"Your honor, I do have an objection, if that's the right way to put it," I offered.

"A what?" Mr. Smith asked, as though he was hard of hearing.

"An objection."

"Okay, I will hear your objection," Judge Hulbert said.

"Mr. Tripps's writing, rather the paper Mr. Tripps's writing is on, has a watermark."

"So," Mr. Smith said.

"As watermarks go, this one is special, your honor. Mr. Tripps here testified that I signed this document, which I have never seen in my life before today, anyway, he testified that I signed the document on June 15, 1863, on a piece of paper with a watermark that reads: ES&A Printing, Redcliffe."

"So," Mr. Smith said.

"So, we have a document that is a clear forgery."

"Forgery!" Smith exclaimed.

"Forgery? How so?" Judge Hulbert asked. The furrows on the judge's forehead vanished.

"Mr. Tripps claims I signed this document on June 15, 1863, on a piece of paper that could not possibly have been signed on June 15, 1863, because the paper the document is written on did not exist on June 15, 1863. The paper was not even manufactured until 1870. The proof is the watermark. The watermark reads: ES&A, Redcliffe. ES&A is a London-based company. True, the company was formed prior to 1863, but the Redcliffe Street factory where this particular piece of paper was made was not built until 1870, seven years after Mr. Tripps claims the document was signed. I may not know much about his *res ipsa loquitur* case, but I do know that a document cannot possibly be signed before the date the paper upon which it was written was even made. This document, your honor, is a forgery."

The dismissal that followed did nothing to restore my faith in society. Oh, Mr. Smith did what he could to revive the case. He shuffled. He pawed around in his valise for more documents. He asked a long line of tricky questions about the document from every imaginable angle, but at the end of the day forgeries are serious business, and serious business has a way of speaking for itself.

Judge Hulbert's decision to drop the case was calculated to sidestep that business. The judge's fancy footwork was merely part of the judge's survival instincts. Nothing more. More fundamentally, dismissal of the legal case did nothing to absolve me from any of the transgressions enunciated in the New Testament. It only allowed me to see the betrayal of Lizzie W from a new angle.

****

This new angle is why I am sitting alone in this hotel room, well, almost alone anyway, instead of at the helm of a prestigious string of horses at Saratoga, or Louisiana or Lexington, or anywhere else men enjoy being rich together. The betrayal I speak of is the betrayal of the principles my father carefully instilled in me from an early age: imagine the violation of neglecting to warn a compatriot against impregnating an underage girl, of failing to detect the charade that passed off the responsibility for the pregnancy to the wrong man, of standing by idly while that man was lynched, of misusing my gift with horses to destroy a glorious filly in the service of revenge taken against a business partner over a blown business opportunity, of taking a moment of Saratoga history that belongs to us all and tainting it. That level of betrayal was hideous.

I'll tell you why I have decided to confront my fate alone in a hotel room -- my father.

Like the sheriff, my father had a habit of hitching up his pants and looking at the ground while he imparted his wisdom, like wisdom was a dirty trick he was ashamed of imparting. In his case, wisdom came to him as a byproduct of spending his entire life working under the girth of horses as a blacksmith. He had a habit of taking the full weight of nature in his hands without fully respecting it. There were callouses that had formed over his mind to protect him against what these glorious one-thousand-pound animals could do while he filed away at their hooves. My father had a way of turning wisdom into questions. *A man might better figure out a way to earn an honest living while he's still young, hadn't he?* Or *You might better study instead of work, do you know what I mean? A man ought to get paid right if he works right, ain't that right?*

I remember those questions like other men remember nightmares.

I couldn't blame my father for not bothering to be more specific. I should have been able to fathom how his wisdom applied to all kinds of situations, but I failed. I know there is nothing wrong with being human, but I began to think it is a problem to be a little too human. *I shouldn't have needed to tell Henry not to knock up an underage local girl, or to keep his pudge behind the barn door, should I? Or that problems shouldn't be solved with a Derringer that can be solved with a set of legal papers, don't you think?*

My father's habit of turning wisdom into questions was roughly the same process underway in legal proceedings. If you are tried in a court of law, the counselor doesn't give you an opportunity to speak freely. Even if you are tried for grand larceny, the examiner is free to ask cleverly worded questions designed to creatively push the truth. If truth isn't allowed to come forth squarely in all of its glory, it becomes a lie. If it is colored by the form of the questions, and the truth appears only in angles and glimpses, those angles and glimpses are really all that is left of the struggle.

I didn't have any faith whatsoever in angles or glimpses, and this is precisely the reason I sought the safety of an anonymous hotel room.

Until now...

I had no idea if the Evil Man was finished. I thought of a passage from Ecclesiastes: *Surely the fate of human beings is like that of the animals. The same fate awaits them both. As one dies, so dies the other. All have the same breath.* I had no idea what was real other than the scratching and gnawing behind the walls, above the ceiling, and outside the window of this hotel room. The raccoons were closing in on me, and they were relentless. I figured out a way to stop Mr. Tripps, the sheriff, Gerrit Smith, Esq., and Judge Hulbert, but I knew of only one way to stop the scratching and gnawing that tormented me -- the Derringer.

####

Made in the USA
Middletown, DE
13 May 2024